No Hand Held Mine

 DITTA: Korean Humanities in Translation

Series editors: Young-mee Yu Cho, Jae Won Edward Chung, and Pil Ho Kim

"Ditta" in Korean means stepping on or over, pressing into shape, or overcoming an obstacle or failure. These usages aptly capture the uneasy yet provocative coexistence of translation's tropes of passage and metamorphosis, and translation's role as a vital site of worldbuilding. DITTA: Korean Humanities in Translation provides a unique and sustaining venue for the English translation of overlooked Korean sources across literature, language, history, religion, philosophy, arts, and popular culture. Each book includes a foreword by noted scholars underscoring the significance of the author and their work within Korea and beyond.

Song WooHye, *Yun Dong-ju: A Critical Biography*. Translated by Flora M. Kim

Kim Soom, *No Hand Held Mine: Stories—Granny Wild Goose and "The Root's Tale."* Translated by Joon-Li Kim and Doo-Sun Ryu

Moon Tae-jun, *Flatfish: Poems*. Translated by Brandon Joseph Park

No Hand Held Mine

~

Stories

KIM SOOM

TRANSLATED BY
JOON-LI KIM AND DOO-SUN RYU
FOREWORD BY ALEXIS DUDDEN

Rutgers University Press
New Brunswick, Camden, and Newark, New Jersey
London and Oxford

Rutgers University Press is a department of Rutgers, The State University of New Jersey, one of the leading public research universities in the nation. By publishing worldwide, it furthers the University's mission of dedication to excellence in teaching, scholarship, research, and clinical care.

This book is published with the support of The Daesan Foundation.

978-1-9788-4281-6 (cloth)
978-1-9788-4280-9 (paper)
978-1-9788-4283-0 (epub)

Cataloging-in-publication data is available from the Library of Congress.
LCCN 2025939809

A British Cataloging-in-Publication record for this book is available from the British Library.

English language edition copyright © 2026 by Joon-Li Kim and Doo-Sun Ryu
All rights reserved
No part of this book may be reproduced or utilized in any form or by any means, electronic or mechanical, or by any information storage and retrieval system, without written permission from the publisher. Please contact Rutgers University Press, 106 Somerset Street, New Brunswick, NJ 08901. The only exception to this prohibition is "fair use" as defined by U.S. copyright law.

군인이 천사가 되기를 바란 적 있는가 (*Granny Wild Goose*)
by Kim Soom
First published as "Have You Ever Wished That Soldiers Could Become Angels" in 2018 by Hyundae Munhak Publishing Co., Ltd., Korea.
© Kim Soom
All rights reserved.
This English language edition was published by arrangement with Rutgers University Press through HAN Agency Co., Korea.

"뿌리 이야기" ("The Root's Tale")
by Kim Soom
First published in 2019 by MUNHAKDONGNE Publishing Corp., Korea.
© Kim Soom
All rights reserved.
This English language edition was published by arrangement with Kim Soom c/o HAN Agency Co., Korea.

References to internet websites (URLs) were accurate at the time of writing. Neither the author nor Rutgers University Press is responsible for URLs that may have expired or changed since the manuscript was prepared.

∞ The paper used in this publication meets the requirements of the American National Standard for Information Sciences—Permanence of Paper for Printed Library Materials, ANSI Z39.48-1992.

rutgersuniversitypress.org

Contents

Foreword by Alexis Dudden	vii
Translators' Note	xi
Granny Wild Goose	1
The Root's Tale	95
Acknowledgments	135
Notes on Contributors	137

Foreword

Original and sensitive, Kim Soom weaves *halmoni* Gil Won-Ok's own words into her tonally astute and heart-wrenching prose poem, *Granny Wild Goose*. With it, Kim Soom captures the violence of Gil Won-Ok's past imbuing her present: "Neither night, nor day. / Where did I go?/ Today there are two of me." This elegant retelling of one of the twentieth century's most painful pasts is made all the more urgent now through today's ongoing acts of state-sponsored sexual violence against women, girls, and boys.

Kim's telling of Gil Won-Ok's account appears today at a historical juncture that would again attempt to deny the truth of her's and all victim-survivors' accounts. Kim Soom's energetic prose and deep-level engagement with Gil Won-Ok thus make this narrative more urgent and historically vital.

In the 1930s, the empire of Japan expanded into China, and the Japanese military colluded to establish what it named "comfort stations." The historical evidence of this now well-established history demonstrates they should be called what they were: "rape camps." The world sees evidence today in Russia's abductions of people from Ukraine, begging the question of why this is so difficult to name in Japan's past.

In this story, which Kim Soon relates here with Gil Won-Ok, this history stands among the twentieth century's greatest—if not the greatest—crimes of sex trafficking against minor children. Since the late 1980s, when some of these victim-survivors were able to speak publicly for the first time, it has become widely recognized that there was nothing voluntary about this. This "service"—as the government of Japan currently states—involved an estimated fifty to two hundred thousand girls, women, boys, and men who were kidnapped or tricked into their "servitude." The largest number—including girls as young as nine years old—were Korean, while many others were Chinese, Taiwanese, Filipino, Indonesian, American, and Dutch.

Throughout the 1990s the issue was a major regional and international topic, culminating in the 2000 Tokyo Women's Tribunal and a controversial NHK TV documentary. The Japanese government, refusing to accept direct responsibility for the victimization of the "comfort women," nevertheless established and administered a "private" Comfort Women Fund that paid some of the women $20,000 each. Most of the surviving comfort women, however, particularly those in Korea, refused to accept payment from a nongovernment entity. It remains a crucial part of Japan's ongoing problems over coming to terms with its history and settling its wartime debts to its Asian neighbors.

The key UN documents submitted by special rapporteurs for human rights include the 1996 Coomaraswamy Report and the 1998 McDougall Report. Released after the establishment of the Asian Women's Fund, which represented a damage-control approach by the Japanese government to Japanese accountability for sexual slavery, the McDougall Report concluded by finding that "anything less than full and unqualified acceptance by the Government of Japan of legal liability and the consequences that flow from such liability is wholly inadequate."

For decades, historians combed archives and interviewed victims and perpetrators alike to confirm the truth that she and others tell. She is one of fifty-four known South Korean survivors of the women, girls, and young men from throughout Japan's empire that brokers forced and coerced during the 1930s and 1940s into a state-sponsored system of sexual slavery who lived in "comfort stations." The term gave impunity to the soldiers who lined up in front while erasing the horror that occurred within: the repeated rapes, torture, and forced abortions. Many survivors recall having to have sex up to forty times a day. Many recall Japanese soldiers jumping on their stomachs to push out near-term fetuses.

To this day—and why Kim Soom's story of Gil Won-Ok matters more than ever—the Japanese government is aware of the United Nations Security Council's October 2000 adoption of Resolution 1325 calling on member states to "take special measures to protect women and girls from gender-based violence, particularly rape and other forms of sexual abuse, in situations of armed conflict." Several additional resolutions have appeared since, including Resolution 1820, which labels sexual violence in wartime as a "tool of war" and constitutive of war crimes and crimes against humanity.

Please read Kim Soom's account with an eye to the present and future.

Alexis Dudden

Translators' Note

Kim Soom writes with stealth. Like one of the anthropomorphized roots in "The Root's Tale," Kim's prose slithers clandestinely forward and wraps around you, unawares, until it leaves you struggling for breath. Perhaps because she seems obsessed with absence, both physical and psychical, her stories focus on characters who are deprived, on the silence in dialogues. That absence, that negative space, becomes, interestingly enough, Kim's representational lodestar when dealing with the unspeakable.

Kim once mentioned her own inability to converse the first time she met Gil Won-Ok, the Korean "comfort woman" who is the basis for "Granny Wild Goose." When she sat down to dinner with Gil and Kim Bok-Dong, another "comfort woman," she says, "I normally enjoy speaking with the elderly, but I struggled speaking with them that day."[1] As if the unspeakable horrors of being forced into sexual slavery by the Japanese military that the two elderly Korean women endured were still palpable that evening, Kim herself couldn't overcome that painful silence. The shame of their experience, the silence compelled by their shame, and the consequent desire to testify motivate "Granny Wild Goose."

Kim Soom interviewed and recorded Gil Won-Ok multiple times, and those recordings ultimately became the foundation for "Have You Ever Wished That Soldiers Could Become Angels," published in South Korea in 2018. Gil's speech is an act of defiance against both the perpetrators of sexual violence and "shame culture." We know all too well what hostility and disbelief women victims encounter when they finally gather up the courage to tell their stories. Gil herself at first didn't understand why other Korean comfort women bothered to speak out or what that would accomplish. But she listens to other comfort women talk about their abuse and eventually decides she is ready to tell her own story, when she is seventy-one years old.

She recalls being promised factory work in Manchuria along with her friends, realizing what kind of place she had ended up at, and the brutal violence she endured. The text follows her at not one, but two, comfort stations; her return to Korea after World War II; and her life up to recent times, when she speaks about her past. But she is beginning to show signs of forgetfulness and confusion by the time of the interviews, and Kim respects the gaps in Gil's memory and language by weaving the interviews together into a prose poem or a first-person monologue as she narrates her experiences.

While translating, we were reminded of Gayatri Spivak's essay "Can the Subaltern Speak?" in which Spivak expresses her reservations about the effort to give voice to those subalterns silenced by both British Empire historians and their male Indian counterparts after independence. Gil Won-Ok, as a subaltern, was doubly colonized: the daughter who went to Manchuria to earn money for her father's release from prison at a time when Korea was under Japanese colonization. Spivak questions the effort to recuperate the subaltern's voice since, even when well intentioned, it could easily result in the subaltern's linguistic subjugation. And we questioned whether we were part of that linguistic appropriation, since our translation is triply removed from Gil's own experiences: she spoke with author Kim, who then fashioned those words into a creative text, which we then rendered into English.

However, "Granny Wild Goose" is also a strong response to Spivak's skepticism. Gil Won-Ok certainly speaks out in the text, even dominating its narration. The reader can hear her voice and can imagine her, perhaps on a stage by herself, talking to the audience. That level of intimacy between Gil and the reader permeates the book. Furthermore, the structure of the text, in stanzas with line breaks, emphasizes both the natural poetry of Gil's voice and the negative space on the page. The topic of comfort women remains a fraught one, buoyed, manipulated, or deemed "done" depending on domestic politics in Korea and global political expediencies. The absence of text on the page, in some ways, represents the paring away of all the dominant verbiage by the perpetrators, by institutions, and by governments to "contextualize" the comfort women. Kim Soom puts Gil Won-Ok back into the center of her narrative.

For this reason, we decided to give the English translation a different title from its original Korean title. We changed the title to "Granny Wild Goose" because that was the nickname that one of Gil's friends had given her and we wanted her, rather than anonymous soldiers, to be in the title.

One of our greatest difficulties (and pleasures) was when we encountered the verb 묻다, which can mean either "to ask" or "to bury." In fact, the opening line of this novel reads, "I buried the dirt into the ground." The verb appears again later in chapter 11, but Gil interrupts herself when she hears the stories of women victims of the Vietnam War, that is, other subaltern women. Gil cannot bury the dirty truth since other subalterns are speaking.

However, in chapter 5, 묻다 is repeated twice in the negative imperative. Gil tires of detailing her experiences to Kim and says, "묻지 마 / 묻지 마." We translated these two lines as "Don't ask / Don't ask." However, we got the sense that Kim was giving us a knowing look, implying that these lines encapsulate the central tension in this text: the competing imperatives of "Don't ask" and "Don't bury."

A similar dynamic occurs in chapter 18, with the word 부끄럽다, which can mean both "to be ashamed" and "to be shameful." Gil plays on both meanings when she says, "부끄러워 / 부끄럽지 않아." After repeated readings, we decided to translate these two lines as "I am ashamed / I am not shameful," instead of "I am ashamed / I am not ashamed." We believe the first line shows the sense of mortification Gil must have felt throughout her life. However, the second line is Gil's protest that her tragedy was not her fault. Gil's change is confirmed by her retort at the end of that chapter: "부끄럽냐고? / 그렇게 묻는 게 부끄러운 거야": "Ashamed, you ask? / Asking such a thing is shameful."

Shame is also referenced in chapters 12 and 17. In these chapters, however, the Korean word used is 창피하다, which has a nuance of "disgrace" or "humiliation." Interestingly enough, the subject and object of shame in these passages are never in doubt, grammatically.

"The Root's Tale" was originally published in 2014 and won the Yi Sang Literary Award in 2016. This short story is narrated by a woman who is in a failing relationship with an artist who works with the roots of trees and vines. The narrator describes her lover's increasing obsession with various roots as he harvests them in nature, fixes them in his studio, and turns them into art objects. She realizes she is in a competition with the roots for the artist's energy as well as his fidelity.

Kim grew up in the Korean countryside and she has said that when she recalls all the animate and inanimate objects from that environment, she "think[s] there has always been this strange, eerie aura about them." She draws upon the "eeriness" of nature as she develops the relationship between the artist and the various roots. At one point, the female narrator says that the artist spreads preservative over a grapevine root "as if he were anointing a woman's body with scented oil. A sinister, obscene sexual tension flowed between them."

Korean critics have often mentioned Kim's fearlessness in her writing, especially her affinity for silence and the grotesque. Kim embraces this characterization and traces its lineage to her upbringing in the countryside: "Nature's solitude is so great that the solitude of human beings simply pales in comparison. I believe my emotional development took place in that world, and because of that, the foundation of the world I create cannot help being grotesque and filled with solitude."[2]

We see the grotesque merge with the loneliness of solitude in "The Root's Tale." The narrator tells her artist-lover about a spinster great-aunt who came to live with her family when the narrator was still a child. As a young woman, the great-aunt was abandoned by her husband when she couldn't get pregnant and was forced to support herself as a maid. When she came to live with the narrator's family, she was elderly and shared a room with the young girl. The girl was very unhappy about the arrangement and, when her great-aunt reached out at night to hold her hand, she pulled it away and turned her back. She rejected the great-aunt and now, as an adult, regrets the casual cruelty with which she treated the old woman. One of the artist's roots, desiccated and twisted, reminds the narrator of her great-aunt's hand.

Though various kinds of roots are mentioned in this story, they all have one thing in common: they branch and overlap and create crisscrossing, interlocking structures. Kim Soom mimics this structure in this story by crisscrossing passages from the woman's point of view with interior monologue passages from the man's point of view. Kim even makes use of different font sizes to simulate the main root and the lateral roots that branch off from it. Silence again becomes a very powerful strand entwining both characters' voices and is one way that the two characters communicate with each other. The various roots in the artist's studio, though not technically alive, seem to possess agency and make their will known with a mute force. The entire story swallows the reader, just as the grapevine roots swallow the artist.

The loudest silence in the story, however, emanates from the great-aunt. Like Spivak's subaltern, the great-aunt has no voice in this story; instead, the narrator speaks about her. She also leaves no physical trace. The great-aunt spent her time sitting alone in the bedroom, inching along on the floor with a shaft of sunlight as it shifted throughout the day and compulsively wiping away any trace of herself from wherever she had just sat. Ironically, it was the female protagonist as a young girl who effectively silenced the great-aunt by complaining about having to share a room. Because of her complaints, the great-aunt went to live in a nursing home until she passed away.

The narrator realizes the artist has betrayed her confidence when she sees that his piece in an art exhibit is a root dangling from the ceiling. The artist titled this piece with the name of the great-aunt. When she sees the artist's piece, the narrator comes to understand that he has appropriated her story about her aunt's hand for his own consumption and production. What she gains from this exhibit, however, is an understanding of her own lineage to rootless, silenced women.

Joon-Li Kim
Doo-Sun Ryu

Notes

1. https://kln.or.kr/frames/interviewsView.do?bbsIdx=1720.
2. https://kln.or.kr/frames/interviewsView.do?bbsIdx=1720.

Granny Wild Goose

1

I buried the dirt into the ground. . . .

The memory hits me out of nowhere. The image of my younger brother waving his hand is so vivid. . . .
Waving at my train and shouting,
"Noona—come back soon!"

I went by train. Wearing a green silk chima.
The train crossed the Duman River.

I cry too, sometimes. . . .

2

Of all the letters in the world, I like "I."
Because without me, there's nothing else.
Without me, there can't be anything else. I don't exist, so nothing can.

There have been three of me in this life.

Things that make you gasp, even spread over a lifetime, I dealt with them when I was thirteen.
When you were thirteen, what did you want the most? For me, it was I. . . .
There's an I, so there's a you too.
Don't be jealous. Because you have an I, too.
Birds have an I, rocks have an I, trees have an I, fish have an I.
If birds don't have an I, then the sky doesn't either, or clouds.
And if fish don't have an I, neither does water.

How many of you?

If I sing, will you sing too?
I've never been to Mokpo, but I know how to sing "Tears of Mokpo."[1]

---

[1] "Tears of Mokpo" was written and recorded in 1935, while Korea was under Japanese colonization. Ostensibly about a young bride from the city of Mokpo who

I had nobody.
I was from the north, so I didn't have any family down south.
Just a migrating bird following its flock, that fell all alone into a field.
I had only songs, so I sang. I'm someone who sings.

Don't tell me to sing.
I sing but I hate singing in front of people.
I sing when I'm by myself.

I'm sleepy.... I'm not going to sleep.... I'll sleep after I eat....

If I sing, will you sing, too?

Does a pebble have a mouth.
Yesterday, I prayed for my mouth to be blessed. That's right, but who did I pray to. Did I pray to my mom, who doesn't come to me, even in my dreams. Maybe I prayed to my father. Whose name is Gil Chang-Bong....
I want a blessed mouth.
A mouth that blesses is blessed.
A human mouth blesses others.
A human mouth doesn't say bad things.
That's just the sound of blowing wind.

I hear footsteps. Is someone coming?
I wait every day. I worry whether anybody's coming, so I watch the courtyard while I doze off.
And same tomorrow, because no one came today.
Flying things, trees. That tree flew here, too. I'm sitting, but it's standing.

---

longs for her husband's return, the song was also taken as a lament to Korea's lost independence.

I'm waiting for my friend.

Who keeps me company. And plays minhwatu[2] with me. . . .

The older you get, the more you have to have friends.

A friend is someone who plays with you.

I play by myself every day. And sleep alone, wake up alone.

All alone, even when I was born. . . .

All the friends I went to Manchuria with are gone, too.

Coo coo coo coo . . . That's a blessed sound. It's the sound of calling the chickens to feed them.

Hush hush . . . That's a blessed sound, too.

I wanted to have a baby.

I wanted to have a baby so much that my face looks babyish.

---

[2] Minhwatu is a Korean card game for two to seven people.

3

I'm not going to speak.

Don't turn on the light. Save electricity. There's still sunlight, it's still bright enough. . . .

I don't want to speak.

Words are scary.
People aren't scary at all. What's so scary about people.
What people say is scary.
Don't make me talk.

My mouth has gone somewhere, so I can't talk, even if I wanted to.
Even if I wanted to,
I had nowhere to say it.
How old am I today. I knew this morning, but I've totally forgotten.
At lunch, I don't remember what I had for breakfast. And at dinner, I don't remember what I had for lunch.
I'm probably eighty. Maybe I'm eighty-two or -three.
If someone asked me how old I was, I said thirteen.
I was thirteen back then.

My color is people color.

I'm going home.
Our address is North Pyongan Province, Pyongyang, Seoseong-ri, number 76–26. . . .
Not that house, a different one?
Who lives in that other one?
I'm me.
I'm nobody.

(Looking at a picture in front of her) That grandmother[3] says she knows me? I don't think so, I'm nobody. . . .
She's the same sign as me? Where does she live? Is she sick? She looks sick. . . .
Anyway, she's old.
I'm thirteen.

There's absolutely no breeze today.
Because I said that, a slight breeze is blowing.

(Looking at her wristwatch) It's not quite four o'clock . . . thirteen minutes before four.
If I pray for you, will you pray for me?
Three of me.
Ten fingers. Whether I count in the morning or the evening, ten. Whether I count from the pinkies or the thumbs, still ten.
Why do people have ten fingers. I'm ninety, but I don't know.
I'm several days past ninety, but I don't know things.
I left home at thirteen and drifted around, not knowing what was where.
I only know to eat.
I only know to sleep.

---

[3] Japanese military "comfort woman" Ahn Jeom-Soon (1928–2018).

I wandered around, not knowing what was where, turning into a stranger.
I wandered around, no meaning, no name.
I was alone. I never had any companions.

I give one finger to my bird, one to the wind, and one to the stream. . . .
I have a bird that perches on my finger and sings.
The pasqueflower said that giving is having.
I don't know what the pasqueflower looked like. I don't remember.
Which finger should I give to my bird.
My hands are small. They were small when I was thirteen, too. . . .
What kind of hands are these. I just have to see someone I consider family, and I'm eager to make them food.
My fingers are so excited, they dance.
What kind of hands are these, all the food tastes different. What kind of hands are they, as they knead.
The taste depends on the hand making it.
My mom made mandu all the time.
My birthplace is North Pyongan Province, Huicheon. I left home when I was thirteen, so I don't remember its mountains, fields, or rivers.
I make mandu with minced pheasant, mashed tofu, and chopped chives. . . . You shouldn't omit the mung bean sprouts. Pheasant tastes so much better than pork.
If I make mandu, will my friend come.
I'll steam them.
Three for me, four for my friend.
That's the way I portion out. If I have seven of something, I get three and my friend gets four.

What kind of hands are mine, when no other hand held on to them.

(Looking at the bare tree branches outside of her window) Even if there'd been more hands than that tree has leaves, not a single one held mine.

Shh. Someone's coming.

4

I'm going home.

Our house was gone.
Our address is North Pyongan Province, Pyongyang, Seoseong-ri, number 76–26. . . .
I passed by it on a bus, but the house and the whole neighborhood were gone.
Never.
I've never prayed for anything.

I don't know how to pray. I've forgotten.
Because I've never prayed for anything.
Three of me . . . It looks like I only know about eating and sleeping.
One plus one?
I don't know stuff like that.

Do I really have to say whether I like sleeping or eating better?
When I'm sleeping, I want to eat, and when I'm eating, I want to sleep. Just eat, then sleep.
What should I say for a prayer?
Eating and sleeping, that's prayer.
I pray every day.

(Peeking toward her room) Someone's in my room.
Who could it be?

(Toward her room) Who's there?

Yoshimoto Hanako. . . . I haven't forgotten that name.

I don't remember who named me that. . . . That's what the soldiers called me.
It doesn't mean anything, it has absolutely no meaning.
I can't forget even a meaningless name.

5

I don't know what one plus one is.
Or what ten plus ten is.
Let's share one apple plus two melons, a song only I know.
One tree plus one mirror, I love myself.

Is a bird faster, is a train faster. . . .
A bird is faster than a train. When a bird flies away, it disappears, but you can see a train leaving.
I'm not sure what's faster, a bird or time.
Does time fly after birds.
A clock just lets us know that time is passing, flowing in only one direction.
A clock doesn't know that time also flows backwards.
My time flows toward thirteen years old, but the clock flows toward one hundred years.

The song I'll sing tomorrow, the song that flowed away today.

Shh, someone's coming.

It's getting dark, but my friend still hasn't come. The one I play minhwatu with.
I got worried whenever dusk fell like ashes on a field. I want to go home, home. . . .
I hate the night.

The night erases. Trees, houses, roads . . . and my face.
Don't erase my face!

Blood erased my face. . . .

Was I fourteen, was I fifteen.
A soldier hit me on the head with a sword, long like a snake.
He cracked my skull, and blood spurted out.
The blood flowed down, erasing my face.
Wiping up that blood took more than sixty years.

The soldiers came at night.
Only soldiers came.

Soldiers in fatigues the color of fermented bean leaves. Speaking Japanese.
Our address is North Pyongan Province, Pyongyang, Seoseong-ri, number 76–26. . . .
The Thirty-Eighth Parallel was created after the Korean War, so I couldn't go.
How far would Pyongyang be by bus. Would it be really fast by train.
Walking would probably take many days and nights.
Gone.
Our house was gone.

My house is right here. Where I am.

Three of me.
How many of you?

I got a letter that my father was seriously ill. While I was in China.
And then I got a letter that my father had passed away.
I didn't have train fare to go home.

Even if I'd had, I couldn't have gone. Because they wouldn't have let me.

It was during the war.

Sleeping with soldiers came before saying good-bye to my dead father.

Father, one.

Soldiers, one, two, three, four, five, six. . . .

Countless soldiers.

I was born in North Pyongan Province, Huicheon.

When I was five or six years old, we moved to Pyongyang.

I remember my oldest oppa putting me on top of a bundle of quilts and carrying me across a stream.

His name was Gil Won-Se. . . . Or maybe Won-Se was my father's name. I don't remember if it was my father's name or my brother's name.

When I left home, my father wasn't there, he was in jail.

"Give me just twenty won!"

"Give me just twenty won to get my father out of jail!"

Should I say I was stupid, should I say I was foolish. I thought my father would get released from jail if I had just twenty won.

It feels like he is waiting for me in heaven, asking when his little one would bring him twenty won.

"Little one—."

He called me "Little one."

Because I was the littlest.

Are there soldiers in heaven, too.

I'm not going where there are soldiers.

When I first went to Manchuria, I didn't know anything about sleeping with men. . . .

The soldiers didn't come much in the mornings, they started in the afternoons. . . .

They said they'd not only give me money but also teach me a trade . . . there . . . What should I say about that place.
I was completely deceived.

But not since the day I arrived.
Not since the first day I got there.

There were around fifteen women there. . . . All Joseon[4] women. . . .
All the friends I went with disappeared somewhere. I was by myself . . . alone. . . .
The boss screamed curses at me because I kept looking for my friends. She was angry, asking what I was searching for my friends for.

I only remember being hurt.
I don't remember the face of the one who hurt me.

He beat me, the soldier beat me.
Not only with his palms but with fists like quinces, because I wouldn't take my clothes off.
I was thirteen. . . .

I survived in that unsurvivable place.

I didn't see them killing any women.

---

[4] The Joseon Dynasty, founded in 1397, lasted five centuries and was the last dynasty in Korea. Korean people were still called "Joseon people" even after the fall of the dynasty, until The Republic of Korea was formally recognized by the United Nations in 1948.

I saw women killing themselves.
Stabbing themselves with knives. . . .
The determined women never survived. Only the clumsy women survived.
They survived and became damaged goods.
I didn't think about dying.
I've never had any intention of dying.

The house was a straight line. With several rooms.
I don't remember.

Don't ask.

Don't ask.

I've been to Manchuria? I don't remember being there. . . .
I don't even know what Manchuria looks like. . . .

There's no way I remember going to Manchuria. . . . I think I went by train. . . . I was on a train for a while. . . .

I don't know. . . . I only remember leaving home at thirteen. . . .
Nowadays, if my little brother came looking for me, I wouldn't recognize him. Or my mother.
Since you can't walk to Manchuria, I must have taken a train or something. . . .
When I left home to catch the train, I think I rode something, but I don't really remember what. . . .
I probably got the train at Pyongyang Station.
Our house was between Pyongyang Station and Seoseong-ri Station.
I remember my little brother shouting, outside the house. . . .

"Noona—come back soon!"

6

Manchuria is north. It's far. . . . I think I went by train. I don't know how long I was on it. We even crossed some rivers. Potong River, Taedong River, Duman River. . . .
It's up north, so the winters are probably cold.

Flowers probably bloom, even in Manchuria.
Because there's no place on earth where flowers don't bloom.

(Holding her black cell phone tightly in her hand) I don't have anywhere to call. . . . No place at all. . . .

After I left home at thirteen, I wandered around, homeless.
I thought I'd have a home if I lived with a man. So, I went with someone I met when I was singing.
This was before the Korean War, so I was twenty-one or -two. . . . A man who lived by his fists. He had a young son and a mother who'd had a stroke. His wife was dead and gone.
I wanted a home, so I tagged along behind him. Not knowing he was a home-destroyer.
Only people destroy their homes.
Birds don't destroy their homes. Rain and wind destroy birds' homes. . . .
Bees just leave their homes behind. Snails, too.
People destroy their own homes and other people's homes.

Destroying a house takes one second but building a house takes an entire lifetime.

If you live with a home-destroying man, you don't know if flowers are blooming or wilting.

And when you see flowers, you don't even recognize them.

I thought if I had a baby, that baby would become my home. So I wanted to have a baby.

Do you have a baby?

7

(Looking at the tree outside her living room window) Oh, there's a bird sitting on a branch. That bird's so big.
And black.
I'm ninety-one and finally seeing a black bird.
I'm thirteen.

(Watching the fish in her fishbowl) I don't notice the time passing when I watch the fish play.
It's nice to have them with me.
Because birds fly far away.

Me, a bird to my mother. . . .

I lived there for several more years after the Korean War. With the home-destroying man. I don't remember how many years older he was than me, but I remember his noona was twelve years older than me.
I am a 1928 Dragon. . . . His sister was also a Dragon. She lived in Seoul and, even though she ignored her younger brother's birthday, she made sure to come down and treat me on my birthday. She was probably grateful that I didn't complain about taking care of her sick mother, who couldn't even control her poop and pee.
That man was such a brute that his own mother said to me one day,

When I die, don't hold my third-day memorial, just leave, go find yourself a good man to live with.

I hear something. Like someone's slicing.... What could they be cutting.
Cutting, mixing, frying, and boiling.
Preparing food sounds like a song, sounds different from a song.
Songs are always nice.
The sound of making food sometimes is nice, sometimes not.
I like the sound when I'm excited about cutting potatoes. I hate hearing it when I'm angry about cutting them.
I hate even touching chopsticks to food I made when angry.
As you fry, you have to think, My stir-fried vegetables are not just any vegetables, but food that people will eat.
Even when you mix just one handful of bean sprouts.
I've probably been angry and made food.
And then smashed the dishes once I finished.

Soy sauce crabs have to be salted.
You have to wash cocoons several times. Then put them in a basin, pour in boiling water, and swish them around. Then pour in more boiling water and swish them some more.... If the cocoons aren't cleaned thoroughly, they taste bad.
I've even sold cocoons. I didn't have anyone.
I was all alone in the south.
I sold them by the sackful at Dongdaemun Market in Seoul.
The hardest times were when I ran to catch the bus with a sack of cocoons on top of my head.

It seems like people don't know. Though they know other people's business very well.

The tree in the courtyard is still standing? Tell it to stop standing and lie down.

I'm keeping my eyes open.
I'm ninety-one years old . . . one. . . .
Brutally tough. My life.

Did I turn the lights off, or did I close my eyes.
I don't see anything.
Good night fish, good night tree.

8

They wouldn't have done that.
If I'd been theirs, their daughter.

There were married soldiers. And soldiers who kept their wife's or baby's picture on them like good luck charms.
One soldier said to a girl,
You're pretty and sweet, and I want to bring you to Japan, but I can't because I have a daughter. My daughter is the same age as you.
Did that soldier survive and return to his hometown. If so, did he see his daughter.

Will soldiers come tonight, too. . . . Please keep an eye out for them. . . . If there are one or two, I can manage. . . . I really hope they won't devour me tonight. . . . Drunk soldiers are the scariest. . . .
I never wore makeup.
If soldiers come, tell them I'm not here.
Say my mother came and got me, I contracted a deadly disease and went home to die.
If the soldiers look like they don't believe it, just tell them I died. That I died this morning and was buried.

What did I wish for.
Maybe to be happily married and have a baby. Who was Maria. . . . I'm not sure, I don't know.

Maria's husband was Joseph.
Maria had a baby!

(Lying on her bed, back against the wall, with her eyes closed)

Mom. . . .

Mom . . . Please help me. . . .

(A round bedside mirror reflects her face. An orange comb, a Bible, a cell phone, a coin purse made from pink cloth, and a plastic bucket are within arm's reach.)

Mom . . . Mom . . . I'm having a hard time. . . .

Mom. . . .

How old was the soldier who toyed with thirteen-year-old me.
As if I were a chick bought at a stationery store for him to play with.
Three of me.
He crushed my apricot beak.
Snapped my wings that had never flapped.
Smashed my forsythia-flower toes.
The soldier looked older than my oldest oppa. Than my father, too.
My body bled. Not my palms, a different spot. Not my knees, somewhere else.
Someplace that had never bled in my entire life.
When I cried from fear, he suddenly grabbed me and threw me into the air.
I flew high, then crashed before his combat boots.

Soldiers, only soldiers came.

I died when I was thirteen, but they say I'm ninety-one. Even dead people age.

My mom's name is Kim Du-Chil. . . . I remember her name today. Since it's all a blur, sometimes I can't even remember her last name.

I'm not waiting for mom.

I'm convinced I don't miss her, either.

I don't know what it's like to miss someone.

We're strangers, total strangers.

I call her mom because she's my mother.

If I see her, I want to ask her.

Dokiwa[5]. . . . It was called Dokiwa. Soldiers brought tickets.

I went, not knowing it was to Manchuria. . . .

With many friends . . . many . . . friends' faces. . . . I don't remember. . . . Some woman took us. . . . She was an old woman. . . . There were a lot of girls at Pyongyang Station . . . girls about my age. . . . I got on the train at Pyongyang Station. . . . There were a lot of girls at Seoseong-ri Station, too. . . .

The train crossed the Duman River. . . . When we got off the train, we were scattered in all different directions. . . .

Only soldiers came and went, came and went.

All I remember was being really cold, so cold.

The comfort station boss was another old woman. . . . Only Joseon women were there . . . about fifteen of us. . . . Maybe there were twenty. . . . Boss Lady was as scary as the soldiers. . . .

Not long after I got there, I contracted yokone[6]. . . . I developed a very bad fever and both sides of my groin became inflamed.

---

[5] A comfort station where Gil Won-Ok was taken.
[6] Venereal disease was sometimes referred to by its Japanese term, "yokone."

They tied both Fallopian tubes during surgery, so I can never have a baby.
I had no idea.
So, at fifteen, I became totally defective.
They sent me off with some man. No idea if he was a soldier, or military contractor, just some man I'd never seen before.
They had no use for me since I hadn't been cured.
Unafraid, I followed him. Because he said he'd take me home.
He brought me close to my home in Pyongyang.
Was that in the spring or fall.
I was cold. . . . I remember I was cold. . . .

I only found out when I got home,
That I'd been in Manchuria.

When I got home, I got a job making bullets . . . to earn money. . . . A military base not far from our house produced bullets. . . . Every morning, old and young people looking for work stood in long lines in front of the base. . . . They passed out belts, which we tied around our waists, and we went inside the base to make bullets. . . .

How long did I work there. . . .

I said I'd never go back to that kind of place, but I did . . . that kind of place. . . .
Tricked by the promise of making lots of money in China . . . me and my friend . . . because China isn't Manchuria. . . . There wouldn't be more of those places like in Manchuria. . . . I thought there couldn't be more of those places anywhere else in the world. . . . A man brought us. . . .
I don't remember my friend's face, so there's no way I remember her name. . . .
When I went to China. . . . Was it 1944. . . . Was it 1945. . . . We crossed the Amnok River. . . . I took a train again. . . . I wrote

a letter home. . . . I picked up hiragana and katakana just from seeing them. . . .

There was an apple orchard not far from our house.

I was going with three friends to play in the orchard, and a woman came up to us and asked,

"Where are you girls going?"

"We're going to play in the apple orchard."

"Would you all like to go work in a factory?"

"A factory?"

"If you work in a factory, you can earn money and learn a good skill. So, you can support yourselves without any difficulty."

So we went.

Was that in the spring or fall.

I went with my friends.

I remember only that I went with my friends.

I don't remember a single one of their names, or their faces.

All I remember is that I slept yesterday.

I don't know.

All I know is that I'll be gone soon.

(Eyes closed and letting out a low, heavy sigh) I don't remember being in Manchuria, either. . . .

I only remember those words.

Only those words.

"Noona—come back soon!"

9

(Around 2 A.M., walking out of the room into the darkness)

Mom—!

Mom—!

Mom—!

I'm sure mom knew.

Where I was going.

Mom dressed me in a new chima and matching jeogori.
She got the long dress and short jacket for me because I was going to sing in China.
A peach-colored jeogori, a green silk chima.
I probably liked my new clothes, since I was young.
We had no money because my father had just gotten out of jail and my older sister had just gotten married, so how did my mom pay for my outfit.

Mom wouldn't have known that's what it was, a place that received soldiers.
She must have thought it was a place for singing.

"Mom, why'd you send me?"

When I went to China, we crossed the Amnok River.
When I went to Manchuria, we crossed the Duman River.

"Mom, why don't you come to me, even in my dreams?"

(Around 2 A.M., almost breaking open the adjacent room door, gesticulating, in an urgent, anxious voice)

The baby's been born!

Bring the seaweed soup!

"Mom, didn't you miss me?"

"Mom, you knew, didn't you?"

I remember the spinach doenjang soup and rice we ate when we stopped for the night on the way to Dokiwa. The soup, made with Japanese doenjang, had chunks of beef and was so delicious, I cried. . . . While I was eating so well, mom and dad were probably eating boiled millet. And my oppas, my unni, and my younger brother. . . .

I asked the man who was taking me to China,
"Am I going somewhere to sing?"
"Do they sell alcohol there?"
"What do they do there?"
I kept asking, so the man got mad and said,
"It's a bar!"
"I won't go."
"Then how will you pay off your debt?"

(Around 2 A.M., below a fluorescent light)

He brought me.
Someone I didn't know.
Who was dressed so nicely. He looked at me and said, "Let's go."
He was dressed so nicely.
Wedding hall . . . "Let's go to the wedding hall," he said.
So, I went to my mom to ask her for clothes.
To dress nicely and follow him to the wedding hall.

Mom—!

Mom—!

Mom—!

I said to give me some seaweed soup? I said a baby had been born?
I was probably going to feed a woman who'd had a baby.

I shouldn't have followed. . . .

I followed when I was thirteen.
There . . . I followed, not even knowing where to.

Don't turn off the light.
Don't go.
I don't want to sleep.
What if someone nicely, very nicely dressed comes for me again?
What if I follow again?

10

I worry that my life is a burden to others.
That my being alive is painful for others.
I forget my face, I forget my name, I forget the songs I've sung. . . .
I keep forgetting.

I remember that mom went around hawking fish. . . . And that I perched on top of the wood-burning stove all day long, cooking millet. My unni got married and mom worked selling fish, so I did the cooking. Because I was so small, I perched like a cat on top of the stove and cooked the millet.
Barley tastes better than millet.
Millet is gritty, so I can't say it tastes good.

I wouldn't recognize my mother even if she showed up. I've forgotten her face.
My mom is beautiful. Her mother did a good job when giving birth. Her eyes were really beautiful.
I don't remember her face.

Was it clear or cloudy, the first time I ever left home. . . .
When I first went to Manchuria, my unni wasn't married yet and still lived at home.
I don't remember who was home that day. Or if it was evening or morning.

I think it was a clear day.
I like sunny days. And people.
I like people who are like sunny days.
Courteous person, clear day, rude person, cloudy day.

Some fingers are short, some are long. If fingers are like that, people can be, too.

I survived by avoiding people who curse a lot, who criticize others a lot.
Even if someone never paid me back the money they borrowed, I didn't ask for it. I worried it might be difficult for them. If they'd had a mind to repay me, they would have already.
I waited until they paid me back.

Will you play minhwatu with me?

If others have one fault, I have ten.

I'm not going to sleep, I don't want to.
Don't turn off the light.
What if someone comes for me again.
I shouldn't follow, but what if I'm stupid and do.
My unni's name is Gil Won-Ju. There are four years between her and me.
Two years between me and my next oppa.
I'm not sure how many years between me and my oldest oppa. He was really scary.

Mom, mom. . . .

"Did you know?"

I don't want to go anywhere. . . . I hate even going to look at flowers.

I'm going home.

I sing songs. When I'm sad, or happy, or bored, or feeling bitter.
Have you ever seen birds choose what day to sing?

At one time, I didn't sing in front of others. I hid and sang.
I sang secretly, alone.
Because I thought singing for others was a disgrace.
I thought everything I did was a disgrace.
But these days, I forget at night what I did in the morning.

I said to my hat. I'm me.
I have lots of hats.

Shh, someone's coming.

I'm a person, I'm a woman.
Does a cloud know it's a cloud as it floats along.
I couldn't do anything at all, so I snuck away.
While I was eating, or putting on makeup, or sleeping. From myself. . . .

11
A Reply

I was burying the dirt into the ground when I heard the women.

"The soldiers were shooting!"

"The soldiers were shooting!"

"My little sister got shot in the neck. Blood was gushing everywhere."

"The soldiers threw grenades. My mom covered my younger sister and me with her body."

"The soldiers were about to set fire to the house. When my aunt, who was holding her baby, raised her hand to stop them, a soldier stabbed her in the stomach."

"My younger sister was crying and screaming, 'Mom, are you dead? Mom, are you dead?'"

"She drank some water because she was thirsty, and her intestines protruded from her stomach."

"I worked as a maid in several relatives' homes. Life was so hard, I'd rather the soldiers had killed me back then."

"I hear the voices of the dead at every memorial service."

I asked,
"What's your name?"
"Nguyen Ti Tan."[7]
"And yours?"
"Nguyen Ti Tan."[8]
"Oh, you two have the same name. Since you have the same name, you must have the same dream."

"Since you've sunk as low as possible, now there's nothing left to do but rise."[9]

---

[7] Survivor of a massacre during the Vietnam War. Native of Pongni-Pongnut village, Quang Nam Province, Vietnam. Seventy people from this village were slaughtered by the Korean military.

[8] Survivor of a massacre during the Vietnam War. Native of Hami village, Quang Nam Province, Vietnam, where 135 villagers were slaughtered by the Korean military.

[9] Quotation from a message Gil Won-Ok sent on April 8, 2015, to civilians slaughtered during the Vietnam War.

12

People who are ashamed of me, of me.

They say I'm shameful.

Was mom ashamed of me too, is that why she didn't look for me.
No one looked for me, no one.
They probably didn't look for me because they were ashamed.
So I didn't look for me, either.
Three of me.
My color is people color.

I was ashamed of myself, too.

I was in Jangchungdan Park. A woman casually walked up to me and said,
If you follow me, I'll make you into a new person.
What's a new person, and
what's a person.
I followed her.
Not because I wanted to become a new person,
but because I had nowhere to go.
I was eighteen years old then.

A fish is a fish, a bird a bird.
A person is a person.

Only people don't understand,
That a person is a person.

I shouldn't follow. . . .

13

The frozen-solid IV.
I won't die, I won't die.

They removed my uterus on a day so cold that my teeth were chattering.
Hiding his face behind the IV, the doctor said,
I didn't do anything wrong.

The doctor put a white blanket over my blackening body and left.

I went to the hospital because my stomach kept swelling and I had vaginal discharge. When I got surgery in Manchuria after contracting yokone, something went wrong while they were tying my Fallopian tubes, so they had to remove my whole uterus.

A day so cold that my bones chattered.
I won't die, I won't die.

I was discharged after nine days, and at dawn, I was so hungry that I cried. I cried under my blanket because I was afraid my landlord would hear. My hunger faded away after I cried it all out.

14

(6:50 A.M., sitting on her bed and looking in the mirror)
Was my face ever pretty?
I don't think I ever considered myself pretty.
I never wondered how to make myself pretty.
My only thought was how to live well.
Living well means not starving.
Eating three meals a day is an unspeakably hard thing for people.
You have to be unspeakably careful.
Because eating
is also using up.

Living well is not taking handouts.
Or resenting others, finding fault with others, or being greedy for what they have.
I look in the mirror every morning.
To see how swollen my face is.
It's a little swollen today.
I didn't dream at all. It's been a long time since I've dreamed anything.
The face I miss disappeared, and my dreams along with it.
That face shapes my dreams,
Those faces.

How many songs must I sing so today will fly by.
I know only Seodo-style songs.

No human knows all the songs in the world. That'd be a god or something like that.

Namdo-style sounds like taryeong ballads but Seodo-style uses a quivering voice. Seodo-style is challenging.

I wandered around only Gyeonggi-do and Chungcheong-do, so I never learned Namdo songs.

When I lived off my voice. . . .

Back then, I never got hoarse, even if I sang for three days straight.

I sang for a living all over Seoul's Guro-gu Oryu-dong, Gyeonggi-do Gimpo, Pocheon, Anyang, Ansan.

Then, I found myself in Bucheon. I was so young, when I sang at a bar called Yeongchangok, across from a brewery.

The only surgery I'd had up until then was the one for yokone.

But when they took out my uterus, they said my intestines had become all tangled up, so they cut open my belly and,

Tore out everything, even my gallbladder, and I lost my voice.

Even if I lost all my teeth,

I thought I'd always have my voice.

Why'd they leave the light on in that house when it's still daytime?

I was criticized for being really stingy.

I don't waste anything.

I don't waste even a single sheet of paper or a drop of water.

I don't use makeup.

When I was in Dokiwa, the boss used to yell at me, look at the time, why haven't you put on your makeup, how can you receive guests with that face.

She called the soldiers "guests."

We women put on makeup and gathered in a wide hall, and then soldiers came and chose one of us.

One soldier left, and another one came.

I didn't think about escaping.

If one woman escaped, the others were punished even more, the remaining twenty-nine of us.

My only thought was, How can I please the boss and go back home.

But she didn't send me home, even when they said my father was seriously ill.

Even when they said my father passed away.

I hated the boss, hated her so much.

I received soldiers even on the day I received word that my father had passed away.

Someone I hate?
There's no such person.

If you have ten people, nine are kind, one is bad.

So, people manage.

Because the nine kind people will hug the one injured by the bad person.

Even among the soldiers, there was one nice one.

15

My body and my damaged spirit can't be consoled. . . . I'm worth less than a bug, but I wish to be forgiven.
Worth less than a bug. . . .

A song comes out of nowhere, I don't even know the title.

"Little fish, you're better than me. You get married, you have babies. . . ."

I'm never getting married, I don't want to.

I like women.

I've never married, though I've lived with men.
I've never had a husband.

I've never felt an intense love for a man, or even true love.
Even so, I know what love is.
Just like I've never been to Mokpo but I still know how to sing "Tears of Mokpo."

I'll tell you what love is. . . .

I'm not sure what the weather will be like today. The weather is so unpredictable.

Sometimes I want to get married, sometimes I don't.

The man turns into a freeloader when you get married, so I don't want to.

Once I sing a lot of songs, will yesterday fly by. And tomorrow.

Even if I'd gotten married, I still couldn't have babies.

Since they tied both Fallopian tubes.

My cross is me.

I've never given birth, but I have a son.

When I had a general store with an attached room in Bucheon.

One day, some friends came to see me.

"Won-Ok, we heard that a homeless woman just had a baby."

"She can't pay the hospital bill, so the doctor won't cut the umbilical cord."

"Won-Ok, please go and cut it."

"They say she's going to abandon the baby."

One friend cooked some rice, another one made seaweed soup. And I made diapers.

The tiny woman lay there, staring at the cold wall.

The baby lay next to her, staring up at the ceiling.

The woman didn't eat a single spoonful of seaweed soup, just mixed some soy sauce into the rice and ate the entire bowl. When I saw that, I knew that she was abandoning her baby.

My friends said to me, who was barely getting by,

"Won-Ok, raise him yourself."

The next day, I went to the hospital, wrapped him up in a blanket, and brought him home.

I'd dressed the mother in a hanbok and seen her off . . . after pressing a bit of money into her hand for carfare.

My neighbors saw me and said,

"You gave birth to a son without feeling any of the pain!"

To support me and my son, I sold corn on the cob, hard-boiled eggs, and even boiled silkworm cocoons on the road to the Bucheon Jayu Market.

My goodness, I even sold cocoons!

I sold vegetables in Bucheon? I don't remember. . . .
Look at that.
I don't remember this. I don't remember that.
I probably sold vegetables to support us. . . . I've already forgotten my Bucheon address. . . .
My hometown address is North Pyongan Province, Pyongyang, Seoseong-ri, number 76. . . .

By the way, is it spring or summer right now?

When you have only three days left to live, you understand what being human is, what life is.
Only when you have three days left.

16

It's already been more than thirty years. . . .
I was living in Incheon then. I was watching TV at home when that woman came on.
That woman . . . Kim Hak-Sun. . . .
I wasn't quite sixty.
She looked about the same age. She talked about being in Manchuria when she was young.
I stared at the TV and said,

"All you're doing is spitting in your own face."

"Will your youth come back after talking about that?"

"Can you get married after talking about that?"

"Can you have babies after talking about that?"

That woman was shameful. She was bitter and disgraceful. It seemed such pride to come on TV and talk like that.
I didn't even sing in front of others.
In case someone suspected my past.

Are you also ashamed of me?

I was in Manchuria, too. . . .

I thought I'd never say those words.
Until I died.
Even as I was dying.
Because it's a story that spits in my face.
But then, one day, I was speaking.

I went to Manchuria, too. . . .
Soldiers, only soldiers came and went.

I don't know what Manchuria looked like.
All I remember is that it was extremely cold, so cold. . . .

I never saw regular people in Manchuria.
I only saw soldiers.

I'm just an ignorant child.
A flower is pretty because it doesn't harm other flowers.

17

I went to Manchuria too, after saying these words I wouldn't see anyone.
Even if someone said let's get together, I wouldn't.

I returned to my Pyongyang house when I came back from Manchuria.
But not when I came back from China.

(Looking at her wristwatch) The time now is. . . .
They gave me a watch, even though I didn't ask for one.
Someone close to me that I don't know.
I am three things, a watch is four.

(At 4 A.M., firmly clutching her old, black cell phone)

"Did you call?"

"Did you call?"

I stayed quiet, but the soldiers still beat me.
I never got anything from the soldiers, and I didn't want to.
Even if they said they'd give me all the land they possessed, I wouldn't want it.

I'm busy. My job is playing hwatu. And I have to write.

I never learned to write when I was young. Or even after I grew up. I picked it up by looking over other people's shoulders.

I wouldn't be able to draw my Pyongyang home, even if I wanted to.

I don't even remember the roof.

It probably wasn't a big house, probably a small one.

Dad, mom, my oldest oppa, my next oldest oppa, my unni, me, my little brother.... At night, the whole family slept together under one blanket.

Was I happy when I was young.

I'm not sure what happiness is....

Ten won are important.
Those ten won called to me until I was over thirty.

I am the happiest today, I am three things.
Being grateful is being happy.

I'll study peace.

Am I old?

I'm the only one aging....

Why am I the only one getting old?

Are you ashamed of me?

I'm not ashamed at all.
I'm ashamed of the people who are ashamed of me.

The people who are ashamed of me. . . .

My home address is Seoul, Pyongyang, Seoseong-ri number 76. . . .

18

One day, all the soldiers just vanished.

The comfort station boss also disappeared.

I didn't know that Japan had been defeated and that Joseon had been liberated. No one told us. I found out by overhearing the older women whispering among themselves.

They said we'd been liberated.

I didn't know what that meant. Though eighteen years old isn't even that young.

I passed the time cooking and eating with the older women. Was it several days later. I was staring out the window when I heard people hurrying by, talking to one another.

"This is the last boat."

"If you miss this one, you won't be able to go home."

As if waking up from a long dream, I suddenly came to my senses.

I put on some shoes, mine or someone else's, just to put something on my feet, and went out.

I followed the other people, like a silent shadow. . . .

There was a little child. Maybe around four years old.

I don't know why but I grabbed the child's wrist. I held it tightly and walked. . . .

After we'd walked a while, there was the boat. A boat big enough to carry about three thousand people.

I held the child's wrist and entered the boat that was swallowing everyone up.

I thought it was going to Pyongyang, my hometown. I learned later that it was going to Incheon.

When we arrived at Incheon, we weren't allowed off. Because some contagious disease, like typhoid or cholera, was going around the ship.

After fifteen days, they sprinkled white disinfectant powder over me as I got off. They were passing out rice balls, so I took one and climbed up onto a military truck.

The truck dropped me off at Jangchungdan Park in Seoul.

Since we couldn't wash up or change clothes on the ship, I smelled so awful that I couldn't go near other people. I wasn't human.

I was sitting there, a silent ghost, when a woman came up to me and asked,

"Where'd you come from?"

Since I didn't say a word, she continued,

"If you don't have anywhere to go, do you want to come to my house? If you listen well and do what you're told, I'll make you into a new person."

So I followed her.

She had me bathe and then dressed me in all-new clothes, from my underwear to my coat.

She sent the new me into a room.

In the room, men drinking alcohol ordered me to sing.

They kept requesting songs because I had a nice voice.

So I kept singing.

I drifted here and there, pouring drinks and singing songs.

I want to sleep.

Mom, I'm going to sleep. . . .

I don't want to talk.

I can't talk, I couldn't talk.
Because I'm weak, because I'm a woman.

I don't know.

I don't know.

I only know to eat breakfast, lunch, and dinner.

And to sleep and to sing.
You can't pick up spilled water.

All I know is that I'm thirteen years old.
All I know is that apples are delicious.
All I know is that there's nowhere where flowers don't bloom.
All I know is that there are more nice people.
Since there are more nice people than bad people, I'm alive, I survive.

All I know is that my world will disappear in a little bit.
All I know is that I'll disappear in a little bit.

    I don't remember anything at all. . . . I need to remember things. . . . I'm not trying to bury things, I just don't remember anything at all. . . . Once in a while, when I can't recall anything, a memory suddenly pops up. . . .

(Nodding her head) I don't remember. . . .

All I had were songs.
So I sang.
I just kept on and forgot, so I could keep living.
I'm still living.

I want to stop. . . . I want this to be over. . . .
There must have been times I missed them.
Now I don't miss anything at all.

I didn't want to speak, so I didn't.
Because it's not a particularly nice story.

I'm ashamed.
I'm not shameful.

(In a very faint voice) If I speak, the pain gets worse.

Pain is all the same.
Whether wounds are to the body or to the spirit.

All I thought about was, How can I forget.
And that's how I've survived this long.

Ashamed, you ask?

Asking such a thing is shameful.

19
To Marvah al-Aliko[10]

It hurts, right?

I know your pain. . . .

You have to speak, even if it hurts.

*

I met her in the train station waiting room.
It was daytime. Not nighttime.
At first, at the very beginning, I was alone.
It wasn't weird being alone in the waiting room. Or scary, or lonely.
Because I've always been alone.
The seat next to me was empty.
I was waiting for a train.
A regular train. . . .
I was waiting for a train going somewhere.
I didn't know what time the train would arrive.
No one told me what time the train was coming.
The train's on its way, I thought, while I waited.

---

[10] A sexual slave of the Islamic State, from the Iraqi minority Yazidi clan. Gil Won-Ok met Marvah al-Aliko in Berlin on May 28, 2017.

A rather tall woman walked silently over and sat down in the empty seat next to me.

I think she was waiting for the same train.

I don't think she knew what time it was coming, either.

Her hair was midnight black. And parted in the middle.

Her eyebrows were crescent shaped, and her large, double-lidded eyes looked gentle.

Her shy smile showed teeth that were as white as squash flowers.

Her long, black eyebrows shone.

Her skin was the color of walnuts.

I wanted to comb her hair.

If I'd had a comb, I would have combed it.

What's wrong with combing an unknown woman's hair.

The train was late. So I sang. Because songs were all I had.

And one piece of candy.

"Seventy years passed before I realized, seventy years since the scary, brutal war ended . . . Mom . . . Mom. . . ."

The woman, who'd been quietly listening to my song, began to cry.

Quietly wiping away the tears with the back of her hands, she started to speak.

In a language I'd never heard before.

It wasn't Japanese or Chinese.

Her face flushed.

Her eyes stared off somewhere for a moment.

Watching her,

I put my candy in my mouth.

The candy dissolving in my mouth, her words dissolving in her mouth.

A round clock hung on the white wall of the waiting room.

The clock read three ten.

Tick tick tick, for a moment her eyes turned toward me.

The train still hadn't come.

Another woman quietly came up to me and whispered in my ear,
"That woman's from Sinjar, Iraq.

"They believe in a god called Yazdan. Yazdan wasn't interested in the world it created, so it entrusted the world to seven angels. Her people lived peacefully, worshipping the seven angels, who appear as peacocks, and praying twice a day to the sun.

"Then one day, soldiers armed with guns and knives swarmed her village and killed all the men. They dragged her and her sisters away and raped them, then either made them into soldiers or sold them at slave markets. If they didn't obey, they were chained together by their ankles and left out in the sun. They were given water with dead rats floating in it and food that had pieces of broken glass.

"The soldiers put a knife in her younger brother's hand and said,
'Kill your mother with this knife.'
"This woman was sold around as a slave until she escaped and came here.

"Her sisters are still being sold at slave markets.

"She's not sure.

"Making a fire on the dry ground, her grandmother said to the granddaughters,
'Even a demon, crying in repentance before God, can become an angel.'
"The woman wanted to ask her grandmother,
"Whether the soldier who put a knife in her younger brother's hand and said to kill his mother, if he repented, could he also become an angel. . . ."

I shook my head.
Is it a lie, or isn't it.
If I had a flower, I'd pluck the petals one by one and ask,

Is it a lie, isn't it a lie. . . .

I really wanted to leave the truth up to flower petals.

People all over the world didn't want to believe what we said. That ten, twenty, thirty soldiers at a time visited our thirteen-, fourteen-year-old bodies.

That they fed us mercury so we couldn't have babies, that they took out our uteruses.

That when they lost the war, they dragged us into the hills and killed us.

Even soldiers who put knives into the hands of young boys have mothers.

Even the soldier who said, Kill your mother with that knife.

Because there's no one without a mother, because even mothers have mothers.

If I meet that woman's grandmother, I want to ask her,

Whether even the soldier who ripped my clothes, when I was barely thirteen years old, could become an angel if he cried and repented.

Could a soldier who killed babies become an angel, too?

That woman and I were the only ones in the waiting room. Even though the train hadn't come, I wasn't worried.

I said to her,

"It hurts, right?"

"It's supposed to hurt. . . . I was in a lot of pain, too."

She just stared at me, without a word.

"Put up with it, even if it hurts."

"Push it down and wait. . . ."

I know how much pain she was in. Because the same thing happened to me.

"You don't want to talk about it, right?"

"I didn't want to, either."

"I didn't want to say anything, but I did. Because there mustn't be any more ignorant girls who go through the awful things I did."

"And no one will know if I don't say anything."

"When I say to push it down, I mean your pain, not your words."

"You have to speak. That's how people will know."

The train didn't come. I heard people milling around outside.

"Don't be ashamed."

"This didn't happen to you because you sinned."

"Or because you were being punished."

"It's not your fault."

People poured into the waiting room. Swirling all around the two of us like fog.

I heard the train rushing along the red-hot tracks.

Did the two of us take the same train?

I spoke only when I turned seventy-one.

20

A song is a song, whether it's sung or not.
I'm not sure if fish sing.
Not singing them doesn't make songs disappear, but singing them is still best.
Because songs are for singing.

You shouldn't lock kind words up in your mouth, you have to let them out.
So other people will hear and spread them all around.
A song spun from nice words floats, has to float.
Lock mean words up in your mouth until they dissolve away, like salt.

(Counting the fish in the fishbowl) One, two, three. . . .
Did I wash my face?
I have small fish too, but they swim away when I try to count them.
There's one fish with a crooked body.
Did you get into a fight? Did you become crooked from fighting?
Have I always had a crooked fish? This is the first time I've seen it.
I don't know, a fish's body can't be that crooked.
It's amazing, it gets around so well even though it's crooked.

"Little fishies, don't fight."

"Little fishies, don't get hurt."

I guess even fish fight.
But I'm not sure why.
I've probably fought, too.
How can a person go through life without ever fighting.
People fight but then don't remember why.

I'm not sure if fish are nice or not. Since I'm not one.
I'm not sure if birds are nice or not, either.

I like nice people.
A nice person is someone who isn't mean to others for no reason.
If there are ten people, nine are nice, one is mean.
I can't watch the fish at night because I'm sleeping.

People are scary?
What's so scary about them.
People shouldn't be afraid of other people.

People are scary.
People are the scariest thing in the world.
Because people hurt others.

What's so scary about people, I'm not scared at all.

A soldier ripped my chima.
I thought they'd leave me alone when I had my period, but they sent soldiers to my room even then.
My mat was smeared red from menstrual blood.
They sent more soldiers as I was turning my mat over.

They beat me, but not enough to kill me.

Because I couldn't receive any more soldiers if I died.

Who tortured me?

No one. . . .
No one gave me a hard time, either.
No matter how hard I think about it,
No one in the whole world.
I haven't made any enemies, I'd say.

I've never had a day of good health. . . . I get by with medicine, with medicine. . . . My life didn't end.
I lived, damaged.

I'm eighty-one, I'm the youngest.
This year, eleven people.[11]
Last year, thirteen people.
They keep dying.
One day, they'll all be dead and gone.
And so will I.

She died?

Who?

The granny living in Japan? How old was she? Ninety-six? She was six years older than me.
Song Sin-Do?
That was her name?

---

[11] This is how Gil Won-Ok remembers the number of Japanese military's "comfort women" who passed away in 2008.

I knew her? I've met her?
Would I remember her if I saw her face?
What if I see her and still don't remember her?
Wait, I can't see her because she died.

I saw women end their own lives.
Women and soldiers who disemboweled themselves.
And women killed by soldiers.
I didn't die.
I survived, even on a battlefield pelted with bullets.
I hated the thought of dying.
When I was at Hamnyeong comfort station, a soldier from the Mine unit came to me and said,

The war's over, let's get married and live in Japan.

I went to get on a repatriation ship, pretending to be a married couple with that soldier, who had discarded his uniform. Another woman asked him to save her baby. Since we had that baby with us, he wasn't suspected of being a soldier, and we were allowed to board the repatriation ship.

The baby looked steadily at us as the soldier flung it into the ocean. . . .
The soldier abandoned me as soon as he stepped foot on Japanese soil.
That was the first time I tried to die.
I threw myself off a speeding train, but I didn't die.
That soldier was the only person I knew in Japan.
So I went to his home.
He threw rocks at me and said,
Go prostitute yourself to the American soldiers.
I heard news of him several decades later. They said he got the death sentence for raping and killing a woman.
I didn't die even in the middle of an earthquake.[12]

---

[12] In 2011, there was a major earthquake in eastern Japan. "Comfort woman" Song Sin-Do (1922–2017), who was living in Miyagi Prefecture at that time, was discovered alive seven days after all contact had been lost with her due to the earthquake.

I was rescued with my puppy, which I was carrying in my backpack.
I just didn't want to die.[13]

I'm happy every single day.
Since I'm happy, I'm bored.
Since I'm bored, I play minhwatu.
Time flies when I play minhwatu.

Not just a few people, or a few dozen, there were hundreds . . . thousands . . . tens of thousands of people. . . .
Not one of us women came out of it undamaged.

Even now, people are being born, people are dying.
I never thought about dying.
That's why I'm still alive.

---

[13] Quotation from "My Heart Didn't Surrender," a collection of materials published by "The Organization to Support the Joseon Comfort Women Living in Japan Trial."

21

Straw Hat

Two straw hats.

I'll have all of them.
I'm good at receiving but bad at giving.
I don't give things, I don't know how.

There are flowers inside the straw hat.

(Looking at the handful of reddish petals placed before her) Oh, they're purple.

Those flowers are from far away, far away. . . .

(Wearing the straw hat) I'm wearing my straw hat, aren't you taking me someplace?

(Putting the roses in front of her) I'm not sure what these flowers are . . . chrysanthemum . . . I don't know . . . when they bloom . . . green plum blossom. . . .
I'm not sure if I like flowers or hate them.

The flowers smell like flowers,
And I smell like food.

Three flowers.

That's as many flowers as you need.

Did someone take my straw hat?

(Seeing the straw hat on the corner of the dining table) Whose is that?

It feels like a long time since I've worn my straw hat.

A straw hat without an owner.
I don't know who the owner is, either.

The person who wears it is the owner.
Because it's a straw hat.

(Putting the hat back on her head) It's not mine, even though it's on my head.
Because it's not my straw hat.
No matter how nice other people's things are, I don't have to have them.

If someone is envious of what I have, I just share it. Because I shouldn't make that person into a thief.

But I can't share my watch. . . . I only have one.

22

Can the fish see me, too?
Fish eyes are black, but not very black.

My eyes are white and black.
There are so many amazing things in this world, everything's amazing.

I tried to be faithful to myself.
To forget myself.

I should have done kind deeds, but I didn't.

My belly gets bigger by the day because I eat so much.

It's five fourteen right now.

(Removing a grain of rice from her sock) I stuck this here so I can eat it tomorrow.

I was born in 1928. . . . I live in Sinchon. . . . My address is Seodaemun . . . Pyongyang, Seoseong-ri, number 76. . . . My son's name is Gil Won-Se . . . Gil Won-Do . . . Gil Won-Sook . . . Gil Chang-Bong. . . .
My son's name is Won-Do. . . .

What's your name?

I say to myself,

"Won-Ok, eat just a little at a time. You're old, so you'll have a hard time if your stomach gets too big."

I'm always in a good mood, though sometimes I'm bored.
I get bored when I'm alone, with no one around.

I hate it when people leave.

Peace is loving each other without bickering. Without hurting each other.
That's what peace is.

I'll find out what the soul is once I'm dead. I haven't died yet, so I don't know.

Angels are people who are kind.

(Looking into a hand mirror with a red border) I look like an old woman. . . .
There's no trace of my previous face. No one called me ugly before, but I've grown old and ugly. . . . I really wish I were just ten years younger. . . .
People relax when they get rid of their envy, jealousy.
I used to get a curly perm every season. And paid 5,000 won, 10,000 won at the beauty salon.
I haven't gotten a perm for some time. Since the hair my mom, my dad gave me is fine.

Won-Ok is over there.
And here, too.

A person has no ending, no conclusion.

23

I'm a wardrobe, a chair, a window, a plate, a cup, a comb, a toothbrush.
Should I say I'm just stuff.
I only know how to eat and sleep, not how to pray.
They say I prayed every dawn, back when I was a peddler at the Bucheon Jayu Market, when I sold cocoons. . . .
I'm nobody.

I've never prayed for anything.

"Give me just ten won!"[14]

"Give me just ten won!"

I went around shouting this, thinking that if I paid the ten-won fine, father would be released from jail.
I was young, too young to know shame.
I've been doing stupid things since I was little.
I'm a big fool.
Ten won back then is more than ten thousand won now.
The jail was right behind our house.

---

[14] Gil Won-Ok sometimes remembers the amount of the fine she paid to get her father out of jail as twenty won, and sometimes as ten won.

"Little one—."

My father called me over when he was eating. Hearing him, my mom asked him what he was calling me for. Because I have an errand for her, he said.

When I went to him and asked, What is it, father? he pushed aside the millet in his rice bowl and fed me a spoonful of the white rice underneath.

Mom gave white rice only to father. And millet to the kids.

I remember father putting his cigarette in my mouth.

I always got stomachaches.

He said that the cigarette smoke was very strong and would kill the stomach worms.

Father was a junk dealer in Amdong, Pyongyang.

One day, I came home from school to some commotion. Father had been arrested for buying stolen goods.

After he was thrown in jail, I couldn't go to school anymore.

Someone put me in the gisaeng training center. I don't remember who.

In the old days, we differentiated between official and unofficial gisaeng. Those who graduated from the training center were known as official gisaengs.

At the center, I learned a few Seodo-style songs, without understanding the meaning.

My right thumb became infected with sores, which meant I couldn't play the janggu. So I had to leave the center.

I thought that if I had just twenty won, I'd be able to get my father out of prison.

So, I went out to earn twenty won. . . .

There was a butcher shop across from our house.

I think the butcher shop lady put me in the gisaeng center. . . . I think she also told me to go to Manchuria. . . .

I'm not sure. . . . I don't remember. . . .

I miss . . . I'm not coming back . . .

If I sing, will you?

I'm all alone.
It's not good for people to be all alone.
You're a person only when you live with others.

Being alone. . . . Only someone who's been alone knows what that's like.

You need to have others around.
It's not that having someone around is all good.
Whenever there are people around, some are nice, some aren't.
My hands are so cold today.
It's ten thirty-five right now.

Don't go. . . .

Don't go. . . .

Just sleep, snuggling my back. . . .

Bonecrushing . . .

The words won't come. . . . There was so much I wanted to say but, now that I'm trying, they won't come. . . . I'm not sure why.

I'm not afraid to live.
I'm afraid of being hurt.

Because I can't speak if I'm hurt.

When I bled from getting hit, I didn't speak. Since I was afraid.

And when my head was bleeding, there was no one to wipe it.
Even though the blood erased my face.

I don't want to speak, I'm not going to. . . .
Will anyone visit me today.
A person needs to have visitors.

A bird's sitting in the tree.
I don't know where it flew here from, but it'll probably fly away.
Because that's what birds do.
If there's no bird, there's no tree.
But it'll probably fly away in a little bit.

Just me. . . .
There was just me, so I didn't hold back. It's okay to speak, ashamed, if I'm by myself.
It would have been hard to say anything if my mother and father were still here.

One woman[15] couldn't speak while her mother and father were still alive.
She spoke only after they passed away.
To their graves.
That she'd been captured by soldiers,
And that now she was speaking for the first time.

Shall I teach you a song, shall I teach you to make rice wine.
Shall I teach you to make rice wine while singing.

They said my alcohol was especially strong and tasty.
It's hard to make wine that isn't sour or bitter. If you're going to brew wine, you have to cook nonsticky rice.

---

[15] Japanese military "comfort woman" Lee Yong-Su (born 1928).

The rice shouldn't be too hard or too mushy.

For making rice wines, you also have to have ceramic crocks. . . . You need two.

One crock for yakju, the other one for makgeolli.

The malted wheat is important.

They sell it at the mill.

That man's mother taught me to make rice wine, the home-destroying man.

She was paralyzed from a stroke, so she talked me through it.

How to steam the rice, how to cool it down, how to soak the malted wheat. . . .

I bought a mal of rice to make wine with.

And then the Korean War broke out.

I was twenty-three years old then.

24

All day, all night.

I went somewhere.

Two of me today.

Seven of my mom.
Even if there were ten of her, that's not a lot.

Did you sleep well?
Did you eat well?
Cute, pretty, lovable.
I hate them all, I don't like any of them.

I'm not doing that.

Give me food, I'm going to my house.

A disease is something that people have to overcome.
You can't succumb to a disease without a fight.

You have to face it.

(Looking at a photo) Who's this granny?[16] I know her? I think I remember her.

She passed away last year?

I don't know. . . .

She called me Granny Wild Goose? Because my name sounds like a honking goose?

She's pretty. . . . She was two years older than me. . . . Not two years older, ten years older?

She lived to be one hundred?

Aigo, please take me before I reach one hundred. . . .

"Granny Wild Goose!"

Since I'm a wild goose, I flew here, *gi ruk gi ruk*.
I flew all the way here, *gi ruk gi ruk*.

"Granny Wild Goose!"

---

[16] A photo of Japanese military "comfort woman" Lee Sun-Deok (1918–2017). She lived together with Gil Won-Ok at the Our Peaceful Home shelter.

25

I'll stay with my fish.

I had nowhere to go.
So I didn't create a place I wanted to go to.
I survived by not even thinking about wanting to go home.
Because it would have been hard if I'd thought about it.
People in a lot of pain don't say they're hurting. Or pray.
When they're in a lot of pain, they just moan to themselves.
It hurts, it hurts.
Because the world's pain and my pain are definitely different.
Because my pain doesn't get better after telling people about it.
That's why I spoke only after I turned seventy-one.

26

I sing even with closed eyes.

I'll sing "Wild Rose" to those drowning in sadness, to make their sadness go away. . . .
That song is so sad.
Is the wild rose sad, am I sad, singing it.
It's hard to sing it when I'm sad, I just get sadder.
Shall I sing "The Shaman's Song," this really long song.
Long songs don't come just whenever, only when I'm in the mood.
I'm not going to sleep, I'm going to play with my fish.
That's not the sky, that's a cloud.
They're all clouds.

One memory.
Out of ten things, a hundred things, a thousand, one memory remains.
But I don't know what it is.
I have nothing to be depressed about, or sad about.

The red one,
I ate the red one.

Sometimes a song just won't come,
it suddenly breaks off midsong.

I might be going slightly deaf. I can't really hear what other people are saying.

I'm bored.
Should I be upset?

(Looking at the wooden staircase up to the second floor) I guess Bok-Dong[17] is two years older than me....
What does she look like....
She said she misses the ocean?

(She holds on to the banister in the darkness, and her foot often misses the step because she misjudges the distance.)

"Granny Bok-Dong!"

"Granny Bok-Dong!"

She lives at the top of the stairs.
I'm afraid of the stairs.
Before she got sick, she ate all her meals with me.
We sat side by side, like best friends.
I can't climb the stairs. My legs are stiff as poles.
They said I tried to go up at dawn. To see Bok-Dong....
I must have wanted to see her because she's sick.
I miss her,
And she misses the ocean.

The ocean isn't just one color, it's several colors.

After speaking,
I came to love myself more.

---

[17] Japanese military "comfort woman" Kim Bok-Dong (1926-2019). In 2018, Kim Bok-Dong and Gil Won-Ok were living together at Our Peaceful Home shelter.

27

The window is rattling, the tree leaves are shaking. . . .

(It's the middle of winter, so the tree outside the living room window is bare of leaves.)

The sparrows are flying around.

Someone's coming?

Who?

Soldiers must be coming. . . . If soldiers come, tell them I'm not here. . . . Tell them my mom came to take me away . . . and that she's very scary. . . . There's nowhere to hide. . . . Someone please hide me. . . .

Please hide me. . . .

I can't erase them.
Nothing erases the marks the soldiers carved onto my body, not even wrinkles.

28

(Staring at a picture of her younger self)

Who's that. . . .
Oh, that's Won-Ok.
If you ask who's Won-Ok, Won-Ok is Won-Ok.
I said to her,

"Won-Ok, sneak inside and hide."

I don't want to speak.

I'm embarrassed and ashamed. No matter how old I've gotten.
A woman is a woman.
I didn't want to speak, but I did.
Because no more girls should go through what I did.

(Looking at another picture from when she was young)

"You're prettier than me."

"Won-Ok, don't reveal your darkness to the outside world, if you can help it. Show only your peaceful and nice side."

Everything's great when you're young.

But now I'm old, I've definitely become careful, thinking, "Ah, I have to act my age," when I speak.

"Won-Ok, good job getting over your pain."

"Won-Ok, thank you."

(Looking at a picture of herself taken on January 18, 1987, on Jeju Island)

"That woman is me?"

"Oh, Won-Ok is wearing blue."

I like blue. If there are blue, yellow, and red clothes, I'll wear the blue ones.
Yellow clothes, red clothes don't really suit me.

(Looking at a picture of herself taken on March 24, 1986, on Jeju Island)

Where is that?

Oh, Won-Ok is laughing.
Looking at her laugh, it's not forced, so she must have a laughing nature.

29

I don't see any of the fish.
Little fishies, where have you gone?
Are you hiding?
Are you asleep?
Are you taking a nap in the middle of the day?
You should be moving around during the daytime.

(Combing her hair with a red comb) Oh, my hair is so lovely. My hair has gotten nicer now that I don't perm it.
I washed my hair as soon as I woke up.
In case my hair was smelly,
In case I go somewhere today.
My hair turned white late.
I don't wear makeup.
I never tried to look pretty, even when I supported myself with my voice.
I just mumbled my songs, anywhere, anytime.

Was there someone I loved. . . . I don't remember. . . . I don't think I've ever felt genuine love. . . .

It's important for me to give love but it's also important to receive it.
Depending on the situation, giving one and receiving one is important.

And so is giving two and receiving one.

The bird is chirping.

I won't marry.
I'll stay a Miss.

I sang ten songs yesterday.
I probably have days when I don't sing at all.
A world without songs is a bleak world, a day without singing is a bleak day.
Hardly a day goes by when I don't sing.

30

If you know the beginning, you don't know the end, and if you know the end, you don't know the beginning.
I'm the end, I'm the beginning.

I'm not a sin.

Who should I say I am.
I'm Won-Ok.
Won-Ok is someone who eats and sleeps.
Who can't be nice.
I'm nice if I seem nice to other people.
You could say I'm lazy since all I do is eat and sleep.
I can't really explain what kind of person Won-Ok is.

My name is "I don't know."

I don't want to fight with anyone.
Have you ever seen a tree fight with a tree, a cloud with a cloud, a flower with a flower?
Fighting is bad.
And singing is good.
Whenever I've done something bad, I feel uneasy, but whenever I've done something good, I'm content.
When I'm content, food tastes better and I sleep really well. And minhwatu is more fun.

I play minhwatu by myself. Because that's my job.

The light's on in my room.
I wonder who turned it on.

Won-Ok only wants to know Won-Ok.

(Next to the fish) She passed away? Who? Old Ahn Jeom-Soon? Who's she? I know her?
  She said she knew me?
  Did she say how?
  I didn't know that old woman, I only know me.
  Her children must be sad.
  She doesn't have children? None?

How did neither one of us have children?
She has no kids, I have no kids. . . .

I say to myself,

Could I get married, no matter what?

Could I have a baby, no matter what?

I was born the way I was born, born into this world. . . .

I say to myself,

I'm all I have.

I came into this world and will leave it after a painful life. . . .

31
A Letter

A letter arrived from far away. . . .
The longest letter from the furthest away.

Masika's[18] letter.
In the letter, she wrote
That, at one time, she tried to die.

She also wrote:

Please remember me.
So that I won't feel alone,
So that I can continue
To live.[19]

---

[18] Rebecca Masika Katsuva. When the Second Congo War broke out in 1998, she was raped by soldiers, along with her nine- and thirteen-year-old daughters, and her husband was killed. She and her daughters became pregnant as a result of the rapes and were then kicked out by her deceased husband's family. Afterwards, she founded Listening House to take care of other women who suffered sexual violence during the war and the babies those women gave birth to. In 2002, Listening House changed its name to APDUD (Association des Personnes Déshéritées Unies pour le Développement), and it has supported more than six thousand victims. She passed away on February 2, 2016, due to a massive heart attack resulting from complications from malaria.

[19] A reconstruction of an excerpt from a letter that Rebecca Masika Katsuva sent on April 26, 2012, to the Japanese military "comfort women."

She is asking me, who loses memories by the day, to remember her.
By continuing
to pray.

I pray every single day.

I don't know what life is.
If it's about eating, I already figured it out.
Otherwise, I don't know, I don't know.

Masika called me sister in her letter.
Although I've never held her hand.
Or combed her hair.

Masika. . . . I might forget your name before today is over.

32

I love myself.

A key is metal.
A key is metal colored.

I'm three things, and a key is three things.
I'm a key, so to speak. Because you need to have me to have anything.

It's a lie to say I love others but not myself.
I can't hate myself,
I really can't hate myself.
How can I love others if I don't love myself?

If I don't love myself, who will?

I'm people colored.
I'm really happy, sleeping when I want to.
I'm grateful for just being alive.
Happiness is being grateful.

It's been several days since I've cried. . . .

I've forgotten a lot, but not everything.

I haven't forgotten my little brother, shouting as I got on the train to China. . . .

"Noona—come back soon!"

His name is Won-Do. . . .

Sometimes I remember his name, sometimes I don't.

I get sad when I remember. . . .

I miss him.

It must have been several days ago.

I was sleeping when, all of a sudden, that memory popped up, and I started crying without realizing it.

I see crying women. And wonder how hard things must be for them to cry like that.

Who died?

I didn't hear about it. . . . I didn't hear . . . A woman my age passed away . . . though she used to come here . . . and spend time with me.

A person is soil colored.

That's what it seems like to me.

Words cause wounds.

Mouths cause wounds.

I choose people by looking at their mouths.

Mean words can't come out of a nice person's mouth.

They say someone died, who was my age, that I knew well.

I don't remember.

I have ten fingers.

33
A Reply

Yestermorn. . . . Yestermorn is ancient times. But I'm not sure how long ago that was.
Is yestermorn more distant, or is yesterday.
Yesterday is probably more distant than tomorrow.

I'll be born tomorrow.
The remaining days are days, just days.

Mom, mom. . . . I'll sing ten songs tomorrow, so it'll fly by.
I'm not waiting for yesterday.
I'll be leaving in a little bit.

Every day is so important,
But I lived my life without understanding that.
Just living.
Oh, I've become so forgetful. . . . I'm so absentminded. . . .

(With her eyes closed and her hands folded on her lap)
I won't do it. . . . I won't do it. . . .
How did I live to be this old when it was this hard.
When I was young, I didn't know my life was hard.
I survived because I didn't know.

Thank you very much.

Thank you very much.

Do your best.

How's Pyongyang? How nice is the Daedong River? The flowers bloomed even in Pyongyang, right?
Forsythia, apricot blossoms. . . . Aigo, so nice . . .
I've gotten to such a ripe, useless old age. I liked growing older, so I kept doing it.
I'm the happiest today.

(Looking at the fish in the fishbowl) The one with the crooked body still gets around really well.
I feel like sleeping at my house.

I didn't look in the mirror today.

People said it's a miracle I haven't died yet. I'm thirteen years old today. . . . Yesterday I was ninety-one years old . . . one year old. . . .

I didn't die because I loved myself.
I lived this long because I loved myself.

I didn't want to speak but I was able to because I loved myself.

And you should love yourself.

You have to exist, so I can, and I have to exist, so you can.
That's the Golden Rule that I know.

I love myself, so I can forgive.

Loving myself . . . that's the beginning.

And I speak.

Until soldiers become angels.

- This text has been based on interviews with Japanese military "comfort woman" Gil Won-Ok (1928-2025).
- Kim Dong-Hee (director of the War and Women's Human Rights Museum) was present throughout the interview process.
- Yoon Mi-Hyang, Son Yeong-Mi, Jang Hyo-Jeong, and Ryu Ji-Hyeong gave assistance during the course of the interviews.
- I referred to Son Yeong-Mi's master's dissertation, "Understanding the Life of a Japanese Military 'Comfort Woman,' Based on Biographical Research."

Author's Reflection on *Granny Wild Goose*

Gil Won-Ok is rapidly losing her memory.

And yet, from the beginning, the conversation with this grandmother, who can't even remember the fruit she'd just eaten, gave me special joy and literary inspiration. On a night with a full moon, one soul met another on a wild field, and they provided each other with a rapture that was like singing a duet.

The I-love-myself grandmother.

The If-I-love-myself-I-can-love-you grandmother.

The grandmother who, though she lived an indescribably painful life, believes that there is goodness in people and that anyone can become an angel.

The grandmother who climbs up to a place higher and more dazzling than the autumn clouds and sings even now.

As during the interview with Kim Bok-Dong, Ms. Kim Dong-Hee accompanied me.

Sometimes she was there as interpreter, and sometimes she showed me how to communicate with this grandmother who delighted in jokes.

Gil Won-Ok knows me as "Ms." rather than as "Novelist." The woman who torments her by visiting unexpectedly to ask and ask again about useless things.

The image of this grandmother, who said don't go, just snuggle my back and sleep, is unforgettable.

I miss her even today.

Summer 2018
Kim Soom

The Root's Tale

Every root has a distinctive smell. A root that burrows into soil that's damp like your armpit and absorbs all the moisture smells thick and heavy. A smell that doesn't force silence on you but rather makes you sink into it on your own. . . .

How to describe the smell of a root whose peel disintegrates as easily as a wafer, like a swarm of insects . . . that buzzes around and then scatters instantly.

Acacia roots have a prickly smell. Tiny needles stick out between the sour, rotten smells, poking and stabbing.

Open your mouth wide when you inhale . . . so wide that your uvula shakes, until you feel the roots slide toward your tongue . . . and after grabbing it, slither down your esophagus, branching and spreading and tangling, then wrapping around your internal organs, your lungs, heart, liver. . . .

Turn off the desk lamp and close the curtains tight . . . so that not even a pinprick of light can slide in.

Wait, what's that light? Over there . . . floating above the sink . . . Unplug the power strip. A shaft of light, sharp as a slim fish knife, is slicing in between the curtains. . . . Close the curtains tight.

Open your mouth . . . more . . . more . . . until the back of your tongue shows. . . . Smell with your throat puffed out like a bladder. . . . The inky darkness makes you focus on it.

I'm going to Cheonggye Mountain at dawn to look for roots. I hear that tons of trees have been bulldozed and their roots left scattered around. I bet they're digging up the mountain to put down a road. Maybe the root I'm looking for will be there, making the expression I miss so much. . . .

I creep like a slug to the roots. Two roots crisscrossing each other have created a hollow, where I bury my face. The fibrous roots spring up to tickle my forehead and cheeks. With their malicious tips, rootlets prick my throat and shoulder, but I bury my face more deeply . . . like I'm waiting for an unfaithful lover to fall into a deep sleep, greedy for that wanton, sublime spot.

I inhale deeply enough to crack my ribs apart, trying hard to focus on the smell.

The fishy smell of raw soybeans, the sweet yet bitter smell of shepherd's purse, the sour smell of underripe plums. . . . That sour smell, which lingers until the very end, stings.

I imagine all the roots straining underground toward his toes. Every single root. Writhing like snakes sloughing off their skin.

Look at that root. . . .

His voice seems to come from beyond the roots.

*

Around summer solstice last year, after the typhoon front dissipated over the ocean southeast of Jeju Island, a heat warning was issued for Daegu and Miryang. He stood there, secretly avoiding my shadow, which was blurry, like a dried water stain.

"Look at that root. . . . Can't you sense how long it's been contemplating . . . its subjugation of the soil, with its slow, slow tenacity? The root must have taken note of every bit of advance underground while, aboveground, the leaves and flowers on the branches bloomed and faded and produced fruit. Birds diving at the fruit probably looked like meteors shooting across the universe."

"Root?"

"There, that root. . . ."

"A walnut tree's roots don't go down more than three meters, even if it lives a hundred years. Instead, they spread out horizontally. Three meters is probably from you to me."

"But where's the root?"

"Under your feet. . . ."

"Under?"

"Under. . . ."

"But where exactly?"

The first root he chose for his art was five years ago, a maple tree root. We were in the sixth year of a stagnant relationship. I realized then that, with forty staring me in the face, I was too old to have children. Whenever my mother and her nosy sisters found an eligible man, they'd set up a blind date for me without asking. I went on a blind date the same day I saw my first root in his studio. After dinner with a pharmaceutical company manager, whose to-do list for that year included marriage, I grabbed a taxi to the studio.

"It's a maple tree root, from someone's garden."

Until he explained, I never would have thought the thing all alone in the middle of his studio was a root. It looked like a tangle of wires or a hornet's nest. It seemed just a slight poke of my finger would bring hundreds of angry hornets buzzing out.

"Its roots were rubber-banded together—like having its feet bound—before being buried in the ground, so they couldn't spread out naturally. When they're constricted together like that, they grow thin but strong."

"So, why's it there?"

"I'm waiting for it to dry. The strands will twist around one another more weirdly as they dry."

But to me, the root was just withered and pitiful.

"And get tougher, and thinner, and darker. . . ."

When I dropped by his studio again a few days later, the root had been stuck to a panel. It was clinging desperately to the ink-black panel, as if on a sheer cliff.

"The root's expression changes so much as it dries. It changes suddenly, like it'd been struck by lightning, and I'm baffled every time I come across it. Because it's rawer than a little while ago."

*

The sour smell fades, then a piss smell rises up like the real, de facto power . . . subversive and suspicious, emitting paralysis. . . .

The root feels really huge. Even bigger than a weeping willow root used to make a six-person dining table.

I don't know what expression it's making, what color it is, how twisted it's gotten. Or whether any side roots are branching off.

I couldn't see it.

When I walked through the iron door sometime after midnight, the studio was filled with a dense, almost prehistoric blackness.

Nearing the root . . . I feel the side roots intermittently surge, furtively trying to push me away.

It's growing imperceptibly, like a line formed by cramming together dots made with a 0.5 mm pencil.

He told me that the taproot sends lateral roots out through the soil as the trunk branches out above. That the more abundant the leaves are, the more the lateral roots, rather than the taproot, sustain the tree. That monocotyledons, like bamboo, have this peculiarity where the taproot barely grows and the fibrous roots swell up like bubbles.

One root casually pricks my belly button as I try to get close to it. About the thickness of a burdock, it looks like an umbilical cord, so I grab it. The hairs at the end waft like a dense fog and tickle my palm. My fingers grope around for the pointy tip, toward a clump called a root thimble. This thimble-shaped nub makes sure the root doesn't get damaged as it grows underground and uses gravity to tell the root which way to spread.

Back when the studio was still in Ilsan, he tore off a root from an onion that had rolled into a corner and placed it on my palm.

"This is the root thimble," he said, touching a speck about the size of a needle's eye. "This is where the growth happens. A huge amount of energy flows inside this tiny orb."

The hair-thin gray root reminded me of the lines on palms used in fortune-telling, so I furtively closed my hand.

My stubby fingernails looked like root thimbles. Turning purple, wanting to caress him.

I sneak a lick of its skin, which looks like eyelids glued together. It'll crack and flake as it dries.

*

"Look at the expression the root's making."

He was referring to an apple tree root he'd found at an orchard in Goesan, Chungbuk Province. The tree had died from something like cancer in humans, and the root was sad and withered.

I was telling him about Mona Lisa's smile being analyzed using the "Smile Analysis Algorithm." Researchers at an American university quantified Mona Lisa's smile based on six different emotions: happiness, surprise, anger, hatred, fear, and sadness. By assigning points to the wrinkles around the eyes and the curve of the mouth when such emotions were expressed. They said that, based on the algorithm, Mona Lisa's face showed 83 percent happiness, 9 percent hatred, 6 percent fear, and 2 percent anger. And, ironically, that her enigmatic smile is due less to the 83 percent happiness and more to the remaining 17 percent of emotions.

"So, look at that root's expression."

Perhaps the most exquisite expression in the whole world is made by a tree root, not a human face. . . .

Just imagine the expression that apple tree root made when it strained to suck in water from the ground. Or its expression when the branches swayed in the wind, when the white flowers struggled to bloom, when fruit ripened red. . . .

I like the expression it's making . . . the feeling of a weak, delicate narcissism. . . .

Did you say six emotions? Were they happiness, surprise, anger, hatred, sadness . . . and fear? So that means Mona Lisa's expression is enigmatic because of its 9 percent hatred, 6 percent fear . . . and 2 percent anger?

In that case, this root's expression is unique because of its fear and sadness: 33 percent fear and 19 percent sadness. . . .

As he stared at the root, 42 percent sadness and 29 percent fear made up some of his self-mocking and despondent expression. But the remaining 29 percent was something other than happiness, surprise, anger, or hatred. Something that, with my weak emotion-decryption ability, I couldn't decipher at all.

Maybe the remaining 29 percent of emotions were thin and indistinct, like the side roots.

When I dropped by the studio again a week later, the apple tree root had been covered with a preservative.

"Its expression has changed."

"Subtly."

"For the worse."

When a root had dried enough, he applied a preservative so that it wouldn't decay from fungi. He got the stain, a preservative commonly applied to wood furniture, at a chemical specialty shop near Euljiro 4-ga. They were labeled eco-friendly stains, so he didn't wear a mask or protective gloves when he applied them to the roots.

Does sadness sometimes summon anger. I read anger in the root's expression.

*

"Oh, I just pictured her hand. . . ."

"I'd completely forgotten about it. . . ."

My great-aunt came to live with us when I was in fifth grade. She married when she was twenty, but she was sent back to her parents because she never got pregnant and spent the rest of her life working as a maid and then, much later, had nowhere to go but a nursing home. My mother was the oldest son's wife, so she couldn't refuse to take care of my great-aunt but wasn't happy about it.

Did this woman, who ate only the radish leaves from the potato stew during her first dinner with us, seem pitiful to my childish eyes? I hated her and felt burdened. The house wasn't big enough to give her her own room, so she shared mine. She shut herself in the room all day long, like she was in hiding. She'd find one spot on the floor, shrink into herself as much as possible, and sit there for an hour or two. Actually, she shifted a teeny bit, but the change was barely noticeable. She'd squat under a window that was sunny in the morning, then slide over ever so slightly, so that by evening she was next to the bedroom door. And every time she moved, she used a rag to wipe the spot where she'd just sat over and over again. As if erasing any trace she had chanced to leave behind. Not a single strand of her hair remained on the floor, but her body odor, a mingling of baby lotion and dried radish leaves, lingered in the air.

About three months after she arrived, her hand quietly reached for mine. It happened to be the winter solstice, so my mother had made the traditional red bean porridge. The small dough balls, which looked like quail eggs, floated in the red patjuk on the dinner table.

We'd turned off the lights and been under our blankets for about thirty minutes when her hand came sliding under my blanket. I had been unable to fall asleep, which is strange for me, so I was wide awake and felt her fingers slide cautiously in between mine.

"Her hand, which looked like that grapevine root...."

"Interlocked fingers with mine."

He had found the grapevine root in a grape orchard in Yeongdong, in Chungbuk Province.

More than a year ago, around the end of last November, he suddenly showed up near the travel agency where I was working. It was lunchtime, so I grabbed just my wallet and headed out to meet him. He'd turned on the hazard lights of his beat-up SUV and was fidgeting near a bus station camera that monitored illegal parking. I pushed through a group of people waiting for the bus and hurried into his passenger seat.

In the two months since I'd last seen him, his face had gotten gaunt, and his unkempt hair had become gray and shaggy.

"What's with showing up out of the blue?"

He smiled bitterly as he stared wordlessly at me. Then I smelled the stale, dry odor coming off of him, which I assumed was from a root.

"I barely remember your face. It feels like I haven't seen you in forever," he mumbled, more to himself, and pulled the car out.

Once the SUV went through the toll and merged onto the Gyeongbu Expressway, I realized that my lunch break wouldn't be long enough. Since there were only two employees and we had to take turns eating, I almost always finished lunch in under thirty minutes. I can polish off a bowl of noodle soup with a side of hot gyoza or sizzling dolsot bibimbap in less than ten minutes.

When we saw the Siheung Rest Area sign, he picked up speed.

"I should probably eat something when we get to the rest stop. I haven't eaten since lunch yesterday, so I'm starving."

He still didn't tell me where we were going. I'd sent him an email several days earlier, breaking up with him. I could see that the one-line email hadn't been opened.

Plopping down my udon noodles with fried tofu and side of pickled radish, I asked, "Did we come all this way just for lunch?"

"An art school classmate heard I was making art with roots and called me yesterday. His parents grow grapes in Yeongdong, in Chungbuk Province, and he said they were plowing up their fields today."

"I have to be back at the office by one o'clock."

The travel agency wasn't in good shape in those days. The bottom had fallen out of Japanese tour packages after the Fukushima nuclear disaster, and the money coming in barely covered the employees' salaries.

"Grapevines are shallow rooted."

"Shallow rooted?"

"Their root depth is naturally shallow, the roots stay close to the surface of the soil and spread outwards."

"Isn't Yeongdong pretty far from Seoul? I have to be back by one. . . ."

"Pine trees are also shallow rooted. If you go to King Heongang's Royal Tomb in Gyeongju, Namsan-dong, there's a staircase formed naturally from a pine tree's roots. The crooked roots grew out of the soil, and they look exactly like stairs. If you climb up the roots, you see the woods filled with blooming azaleas and the royal tomb. . . ."

". . . one o'clock. . . ."

"A deep-rooted tree, like a walnut, sends a single root deep down. You're kind of like a deep-rooted tree."

Instead of cheerfully agreeing, I stared stonily down at the oil spreading in my broth.

My cell phone showed I missed five calls while I was eating my udon, all from the owner of the travel agency.

I've never moved in my life. My parents raised three kids in a house that was attached to the public bath they ran. Even when other houses were being torn down to make way for a new apartment complex, my parents' house somehow survived. Though I worked at a travel agency, I've never been to a Japanese hot spring. I once dreamed of being a tour guide but gave that up after a guide that I was very close to died all alone at an inn in Hokkaido. That was more than ten years ago, but I still remember the name of the inn. The guide, a forty-five-year-old, single Korean-Japanese woman, was named Samako.

As the SUV passed Daejeon and entered a tunnel, I blurted out, "So, you're kind of shallow rooted?"

I don't think he knew that some vineyards planted weeds like dandelions or clover in between the grapevines. The grapevines, which are shallow rooted, compete with the weeds, but when they defy their nature and send roots deep, the quality of the grapes improves.

When we arrived at the vineyard late in the afternoon, the plowing up of the grapevines was well underway.

Wordlessly, we watched the vines being clawed up by a small, toy-like excavator. He didn't close the car windows, even though dust was blowing in. I smelled burning plastic in the air.

The vineyard spread a thousand pyeong up a slight slope. Every time the upside-down roots flailed around, the air shook in response and turned a strange color as the dark yellow dust mixed with the violet sky.

Once the excavator's noise died down, he got out of the car and sauntered in among the vines. He was alone in the fields, now that everyone else had left. I helplessly watched the uprooted grapevines swallow him whole.

*

This root has been deprived of depth after being yanked out of the ground, but if I follow it down, I think I'll reach the abyss.

In front of the side roots, I turn my head slightly left.

And back to the main root. . . .

How do trees that can't send roots either wide or deep survive? Maybe my natural temperament is closer to the shallow rooted. Growing up, I always felt I was standing on one leg.

The day before Samako left for Hokkaido, we had a late dinner together at a snack shop near the travel agency. Normally outgoing and playful, she didn't eat her kimbap but just glared at me.

"Babe, did you know that I cry every night? Flat on the floor, shaking all over, like an abandoned puppy."

Whenever she talked to a close friend but didn't want to specify their gender, she called them "Babe," as if she were addressing a lover.

"I feel like they cut my umbilical cord and then right away pushed me out into the universe.... I've felt like that since I was young. How much longer can I wander around a place with no beginning, no end, before it stops?"

Her sudden confession was so bewildering that I couldn't chew my kimbap, much less swallow it.

"No need to look at me so seriously. Because, babe, there's nothing you can do. Even my parents and siblings can't fix my emptiness. Or my many boyfriends, or psychiatric medications, or even the Almighty God...."

Sometimes I mutter, I'm crying, even though I don't have any tears. Just a couple of days ago, I muttered during a frog pose at a yoga studio, Oh, I'm crying, oh, my back is whimpering....

*

Lighting, melting, flowing, dropping, hardening....

I remember him lighting the wick of a candle, long and white as a goat's ankle. The flame bloomed on the wick, and the grapevine root's shadow danced on the wall. When melted wax pooled around the wick, he tilted the candle. As the flame elongated, so did the root's shadow.

Melted wax was one of the things he found to stabilize the root. He coated the entire root with wax, drop by drop, as if making a pointillist painting. An acquaintance had suggested paraffin to him, because dripping melted wax was slow, tedious, and required a lot of patience. It would be so much faster to apply melted paraffin with a brush. And it was cheaper and easier to use than candles. He just had to dip some small roots into the paraffin to see how even the results were. But he wouldn't give up his melted wax, even when four lumps of paraffin were sent to his studio. He was reluctant to take the friend's suggestion about the melted paraffin, maybe because he hadn't come up with the idea himself.

Drip,

drip,

another drip,

unaware of the evaporation,

the white tears falling on the root.

I heard adopted children, even if they're adored by their adoptive parents, are quite confused if they come to learn that they'd been given up by their biological parents. And that, when they find out that they were given up, that they were "unnecessary," they're eaten up by fundamental questions about themselves.
Why am I here?
Why don't I not exist instead?
Maybe trees ask themselves the same things.

"Why am I here?" he asked himself.

His gaze was directed at me, but his question was directed at himself. The hand holding the candle shook. The melted wax missed the root and fell onto his foot.

Maybe he insists on the melted wax in order to revel in the interminably slow and tense "pointillism period," like a sadist.

Drip,

drip,

another drip,

*

Roots taken from nature were unpredictable. Either full of sap or shriveled up like a wire.

And mercurial as well. Many times, a root that excited and inspired him when he found it in the wild lost all its fascination as it dried.

Roots were prone to rotting, breaking, and crumbling, making it difficult to count on any permanence, and their sensitive, changeable natures made them unpredictable.

I know nothing about art, but even I could tell that roots were a challenging art medium. So he must have been aware of it. I didn't like roots as art objects. I was sick and tired of their image and symbolism.

He had been devoted to flat oil painting before he abruptly shifted his attention to roots. He was moving toward extreme abstraction, with an obsessive focus. Even though he had been anticipating a contract with a gallery for an exclusive exhibit of his paintings. He said nothing about his reason for shifting to abstract art that visualized "Root," even when he declined the gallery. His friends considered this decision reckless. That was why he made no effort to make then understand why roots of all things.

Finding the roots and getting them to his studio required significant legwork, time, and expense. He even cracked a rib once when he fell down a hill with a root he was carrying. But, like a truthseeker, he found a root, severed it from the trunk, and transported it to his studio all by himself. His face became deeply sunburned, and his body was covered in scars from being scratched and poked.

He preferred not to cut the base of trees with a power saw if he didn't have to. For one thing, it was very hard for him to handle a power saw's violent shaking and loud roar. If the tree trunk was too big and solid and he had to use a power saw, he stuffed his ears with earplugs.

"It feels like I hear screams. From the leaves, the shoots, the branches, the twigs, the root. . . ."

A spindle tree, more than two meters tall, had toppled over near the large air vent of an oxbone soup restaurant. Its light green leaves shook, as if they were sobbing, in the muggy air that the vent spewed out. Or like parrots whose feathers had been snipped and, so, couldn't fly. The seolleongtang restaurant was open twenty-four hours a day, 365 days a year.

A side root was growing down through a hole in a nearby sewer grate. Maybe it wanted to survive by grasping onto the sewer bottom. Even if there was rotten sewage down there, even if there was a dead rat.

For a root yanked out of the ground, empty space is like the inside of a dead mother's womb. . . .

He said he thinks there is a compatibility between the "material" and "the person handling the material." I'm not sure that roots are a good match for him. Leaves, branches, trunk, flowers, fruits. Even if you compare roots to a list of different tree parts.

The roots he chose all had something in common. They'd been dug up from their natural habitat, like people displaced from their homes due to a housing development or a natural disaster.

"There was a persimmon tree in the yard of a vacant house."

"'Removal' was written on the trunk in red lacquer."

"I hugged that tree."

"That word stuck in my heart."

*

Three metasequoia trees stand in a triangle in front of H Bank's headquarters. When the trees were planted in front of the building, which was designed by a famous architect, it made the newspaper.

Metasequoias, shallow rooted like grapevine roots, had been identified from fossil records. They were discovered in China's Sichuan and Hubei provinces in 1945 and became famous because they were designated living fossils.

A typhoon warning was issued for the day we'd arranged to meet in front of H Bank headquarters. The typhoon was traveling northwards from Japan at twenty kilometers per hour. Trucks with loudspeakers went down every street telling people to please prepare. As I left work, seeing all the windows on the tall apartment buildings covered with newspaper and yellow tape made me think of neatly stacked moving boxes. And trucks swarming out at daybreak to pack up their loads and leave for far-off places. And the people inside the boxes being shipped a long way, without having breakfast or putting on makeup.

About thirty minutes after we were supposed to meet, I realized that I had no way of contacting him. It was rush hour, and the roads looked like a used car lot. When I finally arrived, an hour late, he was standing inside the triangle formed by the three metasequoias.

The trees, over three meters tall, were shaking fiercely, like the blades of an electric saw.

I walked over to him, stomping hard on the roots that had torn up through the ground.

"How aware are people of the terror a tree feels when it's uprooted?"

"They don't realize that a tree uses all its energy to stand there," he said, instead of blaming me for being an hour late.

"Because trees are standing beings."

"Beings?"

"Beings that stand in one place. . . ."

"Trees are beings who are born and die in the same place. Who bloom, bear fruit, and face death in their birthplace. . . ."

He was shaking more violently than the metasequoias.

"One thousand two hundred kilometers. . . ."

"That's how far these metasequoias have traveled. These beings who stand in one spot, as you said, raised their roots one day and flew more than one thousand two hundred kilometers here."

I wanted to drive a nail into his foot so that he couldn't fly away. Into every single toe, if that would keep him next to me.

*

Maybe I haven't reached my root yet, where I forget myself and just exist.
Maybe I don't want to.

The jet lag that the metasequoias dealt with, when one day they were pulled up from where they stood and sent one thousand two hundred kilometers away. . . . I think I understand their confusion and fatigue.
To be honest, I suffer from jet lag even when I crouch down in one spot. A sensation that can only be described as jet lag. Maybe it's like the loneliness that Samako talked of.
I wasn't sure if the loneliness that drove Samako to her death was caused by her unstable identity as a Korean-Japanese. But then I remembered a conversation she had with a guide named Jeong at a year-end party several years ago.
"Samako, what are you?"
"A tour guide, of course."

Thinking that Samako, whose drunken eyes were unfocused, had misunderstood, Jeong repeated, with a straight face,

"No, not that, I mean what's your identity, what are you. Are you Japanese or Korean?"

"What am I? I'm me."

Everyone looked at her.

"Samako, surely you know what identity means, right?"

"No, and I don't want to."

When Jeong, thinking that she really didn't know the meaning of the word, started to explain, Samako slammed her beer glass down and abruptly stood up.

"I just said I don't want to know! Identity? Don't be so political and serious. I'm me, you're you. . . . What do we need identity for?"

*

Color stain, glue, brush, handycoat, gesso, nails. . . . One by one, as if taking roll, I mutter the names of the scattered materials and implements necessary for the root project.

The first thing he did after bringing a root to his studio was wait for it to dry. He left it alone, as if giving it time to get over its jet lag. Light, air, and low humidity were very important for proper drying, but his studio was a damp, poorly ventilated semi-basement. During typhoon season, he had to get rid of several roots that became moldy because of the humidity coming from the floor and walls. He couldn't afford to move out of the semi-basement, which he'd been in since college graduation. Especially because, in order to look for his roots, he'd taken a leave of more than a year from his job teaching at an art hagwon, his only source of income.

He was basically unreachable when he went searching for roots. Either his cell phone was off or, if it was on, he never picked up. And he hardly ever responded to my texts.

—There was a face in the mirror I didn't recognize.

He didn't respond to this puzzle I impulsively texted one night. My mother had come down with the flu, so I was cleaning the women's bath for her. While putting away the combs and hair dryers in the locker room, I glanced in the mirror and then couldn't tear my eyes away. The face looking back at me was unfamiliar.

As the root dried, he brushed it with a preservative. He used a sprayer to get the preservative in the spots where the root was warped so tightly that the brush couldn't reach and onto the panel that the root and root hairs were fastened to.

Because a preservative alone can't prevent moisture and warping, he also applied a coat of glue.

"It's kind of a taxidermy treatment. If I apply this, the root will harden, like a bug with rigor mortis."

A glued root became submissive. He seemed reluctant to apply strong glue to the root but, unable to find any other options, he silently spread it everywhere.

Next, he put an even coat of thick, clear gesso all over both root and panel.

"If you use gesso, the grain sets securely. Since it blocks any moisture, it also prevents mold from growing."

The last step before dripping the candle wax was hammering in nails.

"It's pretty heavy, so to use only glue to attach a two- or three-kilo root onto a panel is dangerous and asking for problems."

Gingerly feeling the root with his fingers, as if searching for an acupuncture point, he looked for a good spot before he hammered in a nail.

How should I explain the shock of opening the studio's iron door and coming upon him hammering a nail into the root.

For a while, I'd drop by unannounced at his studio and see him maybe one out of every ten times. On that day, I headed over to his studio as soon as I got off work, not because I particularly wanted to see him. Or because I was curious about the root. More out of habit. The light was out and, sliding my feet down the dark stairs, I realized that it was inertia, rather than passion or desire, sustaining our relationship.

Nailing.
The simplest and most profound rite of passage that a root, a natural object, underwent to transcend into art was the one he called "nailing."

It goes through the ritual, which is the "nailing," in order to fasten the ego, which is the root, onto a constrained world, which is the panel.

Making the ego immobile.

Jeong-Hee sunbae drew a connection to the Passion of Christ. She was in the neighborhood one day and probably curious about what was going on, so she dropped by the studio. You know that sunbae, ahead of me in school, right? The one who thinks that trees are the greatest things on earth. We went to her solo show at a gallery in Hannam-dong. She watched me hammer the root, and then said that the image of Jesus being nailed to the cross was superimposed on the root. I thought it was a very Jeong-Hee sunbae-like interpretation. Because she always has a tinge of the dramatic. I think she has a compulsion to confer all artwork with an enormous, special significance. She loathes and shuns critics but interprets like them.

As I was nailing the root onto the panel, when I said that I wasn't thinking about anything except fixing it in place, she retorted to please think more profoundly. It was a joke, but I just stayed serious.

The word "fixation" makes me edgy.

If I'm to be honest, fixing a being in one place seems an unattainable desire.

Maybe that's why I keep hammering, though I know it's okay to stop. One more, one more, just one more, definitely just one more. . . .

Jeong-Hee questions my choice of bas-relief rather than sculptures. She just doesn't understand why I've dragged the root here and tried to fix it, a three-dimensional object, onto a flat panel.

It wasn't an intentional rejection of sculpture.

I am afflicted by visions of him nailing his hand. Putting his hand onto a panel painted white like a kabuki face, and in the very middle of his palm, a nail. . . .

*

Venus had risen over the vineyard when he elbowed the vines aside and walked out. Dragging a grapevine root. . . .

A root was growing out of his body. And both of his legs were roots.

*

"What's a root?"

"An impossible objet d'art. . . ."

"How long have you been obsessed with roots? You, who's never grown even one pot of ordinary sansevieria in your studio."

"During summer vacation, third grade. I noticed a single planter next to the front gate. I put my journal down, got down off the maru, and walked over to it. It was a brown flowerpot, pretty deep. I took off my socks and stepped into it. When my mother saw me, she begged me to get out, but I just kept standing there. I wanted my feet to grow roots. So they wouldn't lead me away."

*

I was telling him about my great-aunt as his SUV exited the Yeongdong Expressway and merged onto the Gyeongbu Expressway.

"She went into a nursing home on her own after about four months with us. I think she must have heard me complaining to my mother that she was scary and smelly. . . . I disliked her so much that my skin crawled when she held my hand. I was afraid she would reach for my hand again, so at night, I spread our blankets out as far apart as possible and slept with my back to her. And I pulled both hands close to my chest, like I was hiding them."

The grapevine root was loaded into the cargo space of the SUV, with the back seat folded down. A side root was spread out, walling off the driver's seat from the passenger seat.

"One night when I was in ninth grade, I got home late from studying for exams at the library, but my parents weren't there. My little sister told me that our great-aunt had passed away, so they had gone down to Gongju, where the nursing home was, for the funeral. I felt a little strange, but not sad. I don't think I felt anything."

This root looked like my great-aunt's hand. Her creepy hand seemed to be reborn as the root and was riding along with us.

"Her hand was smaller than mine."

"Her hand. All shriveled up and smaller than my hand when I was nine. . . ."

Just then, he jerked the steering wheel to avoid an express bus that had suddenly cut him off. The SUV shook violently, and the startled root clawed at the car window.

"Nam Gui-Deok. . . ."

"My great-aunt's name was Nam Gui-Deok. I only found out a little while ago. For some reason, my father still had her stuff. I think the nursing home boxed them up for him. As the eldest nephew, he served as the chief mourner during the funeral. Her belongings were one black-and-white photograph, a silver wristwatch, her ID, a gold ring. 'Nam Gui-Deok' was written on her ID. The black-and-white photograph was of her when she was young. I think it was taken at a studio. She was dressed in a flowery silk hanbok and was staring ahead with a slightly tense face. . . . Her wristwatch had stopped at 1:25:35."

Waiting for a bus or the subway, waiting at a restaurant for food I'd ordered, opening or closing a window. . . . Sometimes I stare at my hands. Because it feels like her hand is secretly reaching for mine.

I couldn't hold her hand, which seemed like a dug-up, discarded root. Or shake it off.

Did I admit to him that I used to dream of sawing off my hand. Just so I wouldn't have to give it to her.

*

Maybe he's a true narcissist. Then are the root works purely narcissistic, for attaining self-satisfaction and bliss?

During the past five years, he stuck with his roots and expanded his portfolio enough that he could have held an exhibition of finished "root art." Their sizes were pretty significant, so he would have to arrange a place to store them, but he didn't worry about or even make efforts to exhibit them. Knowing that various schoolmates sometimes funded exhibition space, I brought up the topic of a show indirectly.

"Hey, who knows? Maybe other people will tear up after seeing your root artwork, like the Korean-German man."

"They secretly hid underground anyway, refusing to be exposed."

*

If I haven't reached the root yet, what is this twisting my hand feels, this bending, this bifurcating. . . .

The root's peel flakes like scales and the flakes stick to my hand. Maybe he mentioned that each root's peel is a different thickness and that the thicker the peel is, the more it flakes as it dries.

I chew on some of the flakes. The bitter taste spreads on my tongue. I chew on some more fragments and choke them down. I want to get rid of the root this way, eating a little bit at a time. So that not a single root hair remains.

*

"The root has changed."

"It wasn't that ferocious."

"The root I found was the shyest ever. . . ."

"So vague, so naked. . . ."

I got anxious every time he became confused and delirious about the root, since it seemed symptomatic of something.

His paranoia about the root changing sometimes got him into arguments in the alleyway with delivery drivers. One day, he had a driver take care of a zelkova tree root that he'd found in a reservoir near Jochiwon and rushed back to Seoul. He usually took roots in his SUV, but if the side roots were severely bent and there was a risk of damage, or it was too bulky for the back seat, he called a delivery van to transport it to the studio. That day, he was supposed to meet a Korean man who had been sent to Germany as a miner in the 1960s. This Korean-German, in his nineties, said he had cried like a baby when he saw the pictures of the root artwork posted on Jeong-hee's Facebook page. He had really wanted to meet this Korean-German man, who had returned to Korea for the first time in ten years and who was about to leave again. But he couldn't find the man at the agreed-upon spot, an Incheon Airport café, or anywhere near the boarding gate for the plane, which was about to take off. Disappointed, he returned to the workshop and waited for the root. When the delivery driver finally showed up in the alleyway after ten o'clock at night, he complained,

"The root has changed."

"What?" the stocky, elderly driver immediately scowled.

"The root . . . has changed."

"Are you saying I somehow changed it on the way here?"

"That's probably not possible, but. . . ."

"You're crazy. Stop messing around and give me my money. You know I fought to pull that thing out of the ground. Look at all the mud on my clothes and now you're giving me this crap?"

"Because the root has changed . . . ," he repeated, like a parrot. As soon as he got paid, the angry driver dumped the root in the alleyway and left.

A dark car nervously honked at the wily zelkova root sitting in a lotus position at the mouth of the alley.

*

"Your fingers smell like preservative. . . ."

"The root was severely twisted, so I had to apply some."

"Which root?"

"The pine root that I found near the Bulyeong Temple in Uljin."

"Every time your fingers touch me, I feel like I'm getting preservative all over me. . . . Like I'm going to be stuffed."

His fingers stopped caressing my neck and shoulder.

*

How should I describe the expression made by the grapevine root? The root that looked like my great-aunt's reincarnated hand?

It was more naked, more unsure, than any other root I'd seen before in his studio.

When I stopped by the workshop about twenty days after the trip to the vineyard, he was sitting immobile in front of the grapevine root. Normally, while one root was drying in the workshop, he would go out to look for more.

I took the milk and castella cake out of the grocery bag and put them on the table. I sat down a little ways away from him and stared at the root.

It was mostly dark brown, and the side roots crisscrossed as they flowed down. The longest one was at least three meters long.

"Is that the root you've been searching for?"

"Not sure. . . . I think I'll have to keep an eye on it while it dries. Since I'm not sure how its expression will change."

"It hasn't dried enough?"

"It has to dry some more."

"How long have you been at this? I came to the studio two hours ago. And you haven't looked at me once, just stared at the root the whole time."

"I woke up at one o'clock this afternoon and started watching it. . . . What time is it?"

"It's after nine at night. . . . Why's it so cold. . . . Is the heat on? It's gotten cold really fast. You have to keep the heat in the mornings and evenings. It's supposed to be snowy and really, really cold this winter. You want me to warm up some milk for you? Once you have some hot milk and castella cake, you'll get your energy back."

"It's hard to read, its expression is a little . . . That's why I'm obsessed, I keep watching it."

*

Several days later, shaky with fear, I said, "It's so weird, I think the grapevine root's alive. . . . It seems to be catching its breath and sobbing."

"It's still alive."

"How can you tell?"

"By looking at its color."

"Its color?"

"If you see a gray tinge. . . ."

"Gray?"

"A gray tinge at the root hairs."

*

He spread preservative over the dead grapevine root as if he were anointing a woman's body with scented oil. A sinister, obscene sexual tension flowed between them.

At some point, lateral root by lateral root, it sucked him in.

They were in a close struggle against each other, before becoming one. Sucking in and being sucked in, biting and being bitten, strangling and being strangled. . . .

"I'm jealous. . . ."

"I want to set that root on fire."

*

One more, just one more, the last one. . . . Driving nails into the grapevine root while asking himself for permission.

Just one more. . . .

*

I had removed my shoes at the front door and taken maybe three or four steps into the studio. I was about to flip on the fluorescent lights when something sharp stabbed my arch. It was a nail.

As soon as I pulled the nail out, blood and a suppressed cry escaped.

I wrapped my foot with a towel and, while waiting for the bleeding to stop, I clenched the nail tightly in my hand.

The nail that pierced my foot had been hammered into the grapevine root.

He stuck sixty-nine nails into it.

*

The root, which had survived the nailing ritual, was fixed firmly onto a panel. The panel, measuring ten by twenty meters, hung along an entire wall of the studio.

I unwittingly backed away . . . thinking the root, arising from the panel as if it were stretching and disgorging the sixty-nine nails with a sigh, was about to attack me.

The lateral roots flowed in unison toward four o'clock. He used the nails to make them all flow in the same direction. And that made the grapevine root's expression strangely contorted.

It wasn't my great-aunt's reincarnated hand anymore.

"I'm going to exhibit the grapevine root."

He said that Jeong-Hee had contacted him because she was planning a nine-person exhibition at a new gallery.

"I think that root's going to swallow you up."

"Your whole existence. . . ."

*

The blood red color snaked around, lustrous, so is that why I thought of dismembered cricket legs? The lindera tree side root was a worm living in moist, shady dirt.

He had fallen asleep with his feet toward the lindera tree root. His toes were covered by root hairs, which created the illusion that the roots were growing out of his feet.

I went over with a pair of scissors. Sitting down right in front of the root, I took the scissors to the antenna-like root hairs, which were trembling delicately.

When he woke up, the area around his feet was littered with snipped root hairs. He looked bewildered and dazed for a moment, and his bloodshot eyes flickered.

My hand, still holding the scissors, was shaking.

"What have you done?"

"That worm was going to eat you. . . ."

"That worm. . . ."

I couldn't see the expression that the lindera root, lopped back by my impulsive pruning, was making. Because it was a repulsive, creepy bug, stamped with the impression, rather than the expression, of a bug.

*

I grope around for the innermost root, feeling like I'm pursuing the case of a mysterious disappearance.

He visited my dreams, too. He was a complete stranger to me, but I knew that the man in my dream, wearing a raincoat and lost in thought, was him.

Maybe I was daydreaming about the ancient capital. After graduating from college, I lived in Gyeongju for more than a year, renting a room from an old woman who lived alone. That's where I saw a green plum tree being repotted.

It had been sprinkling all day long. I sat on the maru, eating the noodles the old landlady had made for me and watching a man transfer the tree to a planter.

I remember the smell of the damp earth, of the noodles in beef broth, of beans cooking. One household in that alleyway sold homemade cheonggukjang, so the smell of cooked soybeans filled the air.

The man wore a mugwort-green raincoat and boots. And his back was slightly bent.

The sound of the shovel being pushed into the flower garden's moist soil, over by the stone wall, is clear.

Have you ever heard a dull kitchen knife being sharpened on a whetstone? It sounded like that.

The man dug a trench around the green plum tree.

The hood on his raincoat was up, so I couldn't see his face fully. In the courtyard, the dogwood's white flowers seemed to be made from waterproof paper, since they didn't seem to get wet from the rain, or rot, or wilt. . . .

The old landlady sat curled up like a cat at one end of the maru and said to herself, I'll send it to my oldest daughter, in Ulsan. Every time her lawyer husband visits, he was so greedy for it, I couldn't keep pretending to not notice.

The damp earth smelled sweet. It was teeming with bugs, and I realized then that it smelled sweet from all the decomposing bodies.

I wanted to eat the dirt. I was curious about that taste you get only after you're dead.

My eyes kept closing. I was surrounded by the smell of the dirt and an irresistible sleep swept over me. When I woke up, the man, the green plum tree, and the old landlady were all gone and I was alone at the house.

I got down from the maru. I went to the garden and looked down at where the tree had been. There was a hole about sixty centimeters in diameter. The man's large footprints were all around it.

I stepped into the hole.

It felt different from when I put my feet into the empty flowerpot as a child.

I heard the sound of sharp teeth sprouting from my toes and eating the dirt in the hole. And the ants, wood lice, crickets, earthworms that lived in the dirt. . . .

I visited Gyeongju again the following year and heard from the old landlady that the man had passed away from liver cancer.

I asked her about the green plum tree. She said that the soil wasn't right at her daughter's house, so it withered and died.

He appears in my dreams all the time now, wearing a shiny, wet, mugwort-green raincoat, as always.

He feels like an absolute being to me. One I can never overcome. Why am I so afraid of someone who died a long time ago?

The man in the raincoat appeared in my dreams the night the travel agency where I'd worked for twelve years went out of business, unable to overcome the market slump. The head of the travel agency, who was over seventy years old, said that he would arrange his affairs in Seoul and then start a new life down in Hwasun. I was taken aback because I knew that Gimcheon, in Gyeongbuk Province, was his hometown.

"Why Hwasun?"

"We thought about it, and there's no reason to stay in Seoul now that the kids are all grown. When I said, let's go live somewhere quiet, my wife, who is normally indifferent, said Hwasun. More than a decade ago, she took a quick look around on her way to Yeosu with some high school friends. She liked how it felt, so we went there together and found a farmhouse that we liked. . . . I'm tired of Seoul. I came here when I was twenty, so I've lived here for more than fifty years. I've had enough being somewhere I don't really want to be. I don't want to stay another day."

"Aren't you afraid?" I couldn't help asking because I thought it reckless that he was taking up farming, when he'd never planted even a single lettuce seed.

"Of course I'm nervous since we won't know anyone there. I mean, I could get cancer or something at any point. But before we signed the contract, my wife and I walked out to the field that comes with the farmhouse. We stood there soaking up the sun for about twenty minutes. That's when my body got all tingly, like all the coagulated blood was dissolving and circulating, reviving me."

I took the subway home from work as usual that day. After a late-ish dinner, I helped clean the bathhouse. Our bathhouse, which was older than me, had been overshadowed by large, modern bathhouses equipped with saunas, and only elderly regulars still came. My parents didn't employ any workers but worked hard to do everything themselves, barely scraping by.

Stepping into a drained, empty tub, I murmured, in spite of myself, Why am I here. . . .

*

The art gallery was converted from a traditional hanok-style house near the Gyeongbok Palace subway station.

I stopped by on the last day of the exhibition. His grapevine root was disgusting and unappealing, and I had already sent a second email breaking up with him. I was hoping he might be there, but he wasn't.

His work was displayed in the remodeled kitchen. Instead of stepping inside, I stood there, paralyzed.

The root was hanging in midair. (It had been stuck, like a leech, onto a panel until three days before the opening.) Its trembling shadow flowed from the ceiling and walls to the floor.

"Nam Gui-Deok."

That was the title. I couldn't tear my eyes away from the card, which was stuck on the wall to the right of the entrance, with "Nam Gui-Deok" written on it like a name tag.

Stepping into the grapevine root's overflowing shadow, I finally realized. During the long, long nights, when my great-aunt lifted up my blanket and groped around for something to grasp, it wasn't my hand she was after. It was a handful of earth, earth to harbor her, after she'd been dug up and flung into empty space.

I think I know now. The face superimposed onto the face in the mirror, the face I stared so intently at, was none other than my great-aunt's.

Walking to the subway station from the gallery, I suddenly missed her hand. In all my remaining days, I doubt another hand will search out mine as fervently as hers did.

*

The early morning light filters in through the curtains. As a blue light suffuses the workshop, where not a single speck of sunlight had shone before, the root's outline gradually emerges.

One root rises up like the horizon. One side root climbs over another side root, tinged with green light.

And above that one, yet another side root. . . .

"There's something I couldn't tell you before."

"Do you know what my great-aunt was grabbing for in the final moments of her life? My hand. When she passed away in the nursing home, I felt it all, her hand flying into my room, lifting up my blanket, groping around. Groping, searching, feeling around for my hand. . . ."

Acknowledgments

Joon-Li and Doo-Sun would like to thank author Kim Soom for the honor and pleasure of working with her and her writing. We also thank Rosa Han, of HAN Agency Co., Korea, for her assistance with our many questions. We are also very grateful to the Daesan Foundation for its support toward the publication of "Granny Wild Goose." Finally, we would like to thank Professor Young-mee Yu Cho for including *No Hand Held Mine* in the DITTA: Korean Humanities in Translation series.

Notes on Contributors

Amazingly prolific, KIM SOOM spans genres, writing novels, graphic novels, and literary nonfiction. In her fourteen novels and six short story collections, she writes of the underprivileged and marginalized, exposing the underbelly of society with sensitivity and precision. KIM SOOM has won every major Korean literary award, including the Daesan Literary Award, the Hyundae Munhak Award, the Yi Sang Literary Award, Heo Gyun Literary Award, and the Tong-ni Literature Prize. In 2020, she received the Dong-In Literary Award. Kim has been translated into English, Japanese, and German.

JOON-LI KIM holds an undergraduate degree in psychology from Yale University and a master's in English and creative writing from New York University. She is a freelance writer and an editor of academic research papers, novels, and memoirs.

DOO-SUN RYU, professor emeritus in the Department of English Language and Literature, Seoul National University, specializes in twentieth-century English literature. He is also interested in postcolonial studies. He received his PhD in English from New York University after receiving his BA and MA from SNU. His publications include *D.H. Lawrence's The Rainbow and Women in Love: A Critical Study* (Peter Lang) and "Implications of Lawrence's Protest: 'I am so tired of being told that I want mankind to go back to the condition of savages'" (*D.H. Lawrence Studies*).

ALEXIS DUDDEN is professor of history at the University of Connecticut and visiting professor of Japanese studies at the National University of Singapore. Her research and teaching focus on the disputed legacies of the Japanese empire and multinational efforts to deny the histories involved.